READ ME

& Other
Ghost Stories

Text & Illustrations
Copyright © 2020 by Keith Minnion

ISBN 978-1-951510-68-8

Book design and cover by Keith Minnion

For information address Crossroad Press at
141 Brayden Dr., Hertford, NC 27944.

A Macabre Ink Production – Macabre Ink is an imprint of
Crossroad Press.
www.crossroadpress.com

Crossroad Press Trade Edition
2020

READ ME

& Other Ghost Stories

KEITH MINNION

This one is for
Jake & Madison

Contents

Read Me

A Novella

Tuesday, December 3, 1974

Detective Second-Grade Edward Schuyler, from the County Barracks, followed the tire tracks in the snow from the university's utility garages through what looked in the dark like virgin Catskill woods, to the scene of the crime.

Town uniforms were assisting his troopers stringing generator lights, but the path the cruisers had blazed made it easy for his unmarked Plymouth. Ahead he saw blue and red cruiser lights flashing, flashlights careening, and several headlight sets aimed together, spotlighting a mature maple tree at the far edge of a small orchard.

He parked next to the County CSU van. He counted two county cruisers, one from the town police, and two more from campus security. *Welcome to the party, Eddie.* They were parked to the side, between even rows of apple trees. Definitely an orchard. Shirley in Dispatch had mentioned that. "It's at the south end of the campus, Detective. Part of the agricultural college. You can't miss it."

He popped a final marshmallow into his mouth—his wife rationed him to five a day—and heaved the Plymouth's door open. As he did so the power generator coughed to life, and by the time he reached the knot of county troopers, town uniforms and campus security police, the tripod floods had come on.

The troopers nodded to him, and the others made room. He scanned their somber faces. "Who's got it?"

One of the troopers—Williams? Wilhelm? Something like that—pointed to a campus security corporal: short, beefy, with a stiff crew-cut and a face red from the cold. "I'm Bill Mallon, Detective," he said. "I discovered the body, called it in, then secured the scene."

Schuyler nodded. "I'll follow you."

Mallon led him along a narrow path of footprints in the new snow to a point about ten feet from the tree and the body hanging from it, well inside the bubble, the no-man's land of the crime scene itself. The CSU team—Jerry Anderson and Susan Matthews—stood nearby, cooling their heels. Schuyler looked to them. "M.E.?"

"On his way," Matthews said. "Coming from another one in Kingston."

"We already did a perimeter and ground search." Anderson gestured to the north side of the bubble. "We found prints from over there."

"How many?"

"Looks like just the one. One set coming, none leaving."

"Any kind of ID?"

"We found a canvas backpack by the tree." Matthews pointed a thumb back to their van. "Bagged and tagged. No wallet in it, though. No university ID."

Schuyler took out his flashlight and focused it on the dead boy. Hung by the neck with what looked like common clothesline. The neck definitely looked broken, and extended. Death had probably been quick. He was at least ten feet off the ground, and the clothesline went up another ten, tied to one of the larger limbs. He looked nineteen or twenty, shoulder-length light-brown hair, medium build, maybe five-nine or ten and a hundred-forty, dark orange coat, jeans, tennis shoes. The jeans were soaked at the crotch and down one leg, and probably loaded with shit. Paint stains on the jeans as well. Did the university have an art college?

He drew in a long breath, then let it out through his nose. He re-pocketed the flashlight.

Beside him, Corporal Mallon swallowed loudly. "I wish we could just take him down."

"That's the medical examiner's call, Corporal. This was all you saw?"

"Yes sir. No one else here. I only found him because I saw

the coat through the trees. The color stood out."

"You were on patrol?"

"Yes sir. I come down this way at least twice on my shift. I saw him the second swing through."

"When was that?"

"I confirmed it at 10:35, so I first saw the coat a few minutes before that."

"You accessed the scene from the south, right? From the garages?"

"Yes sir. I didn't want to contaminate the north side, where he probably entered from."

"Good."

"The kids use the orchard to party sometimes."

"Even in the snow?"

"The weather doesn't phase them when they're drunk or high."

Schuyler returned his attention to the dead boy. A light breeze made him swing, ever so slightly.

He turned around. "Where the hell's the goddamn M.E.?"

Tuesday, February 9, 1960

Cy remembered the crash, the shock, the screeching, tearing metal...but most of all he remembered the explosion of pain: burning, ragged, everywhere...and the weeping, his mother, weeping through the moaning wind as the snowstorm blew, unconcerned, about them. And when the wind finally faded: nothing; quiet. As the cold crept in with the drifting snow, he remembered thinking: *Why is it snowing inside our car?* And: *Is Daddy sleeping too?*

1

Sunday, September 29, 1974

The Rackham School of Medicine, the university's oldest college, crouched over them like some ivy-crusted beast.

"That's quite a scar you have there," Ben said.

Cy's tee shirt had hiked up; he pulled it down, then the stiff intern smock. "Sixty-seven stitches."

"Wow. Should I ask?"

"Car accident."

"Double wow. Were you driving?"

"I was five."

"Oh." Ben stopped. "Oh."

Cy read his friend's expression–that he guessed the story behind the scar, something better left unsaid–and decided to let it go.

"You also get a surgeon's mask." Ben handed him one, then held up his own. "I usually pull both elastic bands over and wear it on my shoulder or under my chin until I need it." He demonstrated. "It helps with the smell." He reached into a box and pulled out latex gloves. "You're not going to touch anything, so you won't need these."

"I couldn't draw anything wearing them anyway." Cy looked toward the door to the hallway. "Are you sure we won't get caught?"

"No worries. Nobody ever comes down here on a Sunday night. There's just the cadavers and the work-study security nerd." Ben waved the gloves. "And that would be me." He dipped into his lab coat pocket and brought out a ring of keys. "You get to play Leonardo Da Vinci, and I risk a yelling at or a slap on the wrist. Maybe a warning letter in my file, or a suspension if I'm really lucky."

"So no big deal, then," Cy said.

Ben cackled. "You ready?"

Cy slung his old Army surplus rucksack over one shoulder. "Lead on."

They left the morgue office through a set of oak and wire glass doors, and went down a shadowed corridor lined with metal cabinets and open shelves. The shelves were crowded with cartons, bottles and God-knew-what-else shrouded in grey plastic dust-covers. Ben glanced back, "What did you have for dinner?"

"Nothing. You told me not to, remember?"

"You'll thank me."

They passed through yet one more set of doors, metal this time, that opened and closed on rubber gaskets, and the smell hit Cy in the face like a slap: cold meat, cold sweat, with something acidic and sour underlying it all. He had a sudden urge to vomit, but swallowed it back.

"Jesus," he said.

Ben grinned. "Told you."

The corridor before them offered three doors down its short length. Ben pointed. "Those two are to the surgery theaters, but we're not going there." He pushed the remaining door open. "We're going in here."

The room they entered was large and square, with soapstone counters and glass-doored upper cabinets along all four walls. Four permanently mounted dissection drain tables took up the center of the room, with several empty gurneys parked nearby. It was cold as well, refrigerator cold. Blue shadows predominated. Ben flipped some wall switches, and Cy blinked in the sudden glare. One of the tables had something under a pink sheet.

"Who's that?"

"Fred. Or part of him, anyway."

"Part of him?"

Ben nodded. "We're down to appendages with poor old Fred. The freshness date's expired on all the good bits."

"Oh boy." Cy swallowed another lump.

Ben folded the sheet back, revealing a neatly sawn cross-section of a hip joint. The skin had been pinned, and the fatty layer removed, exposing the major muscles and vessels. Ben pointed, "Rectus femoris, vastus lateralis, vastus medialis." He grabbed a large tweezers and moved something, "And that's his sartorious."

"What's that crusty brown stuff around the bone?"

"Rheumatoid arthritis. He had it really bad, poor bastard. You should have seen his hands."

Something banged, somewhere beyond the room.

"Oh shit." Ben was in sudden motion, grabbing a gurney, then a neatly folded sheet, flapping it open. "Get in the gurney!"

"What?"

"In the gurney! The bottom part, you'll fit. Now!"

Cy crouched and crawled onto the gurney's bottom shelf. As the sheet settled around him, he heard another bang, louder, closer. Ben got the gurney moving, and bumped it up against a counter.

Cy heard a door open, then a voice, middle-aged, rough from smoking, with a vague eastern European accent. "Mr. Roth! I find you at last."

"Yes sir. You wanted something?"

"My notes. My lecture notes for tomorrow. I left them—"

Someone nudged the gurney. "What is this?"

Oh shit.

"That's mine, um, my backpack."

"Since when do we allow personal items anywhere but in the offices, eh? And this, this pack of yours looks positively filthy."

"I'm sorry Dr. Baylor. You're right. I'll take it back right now."

"We will both go. My notes. I am sure I left them in the Theater One office. You will help me look."

"Yes sir."

Cy heard the sound of shuffling feet, the snap of the light switch, and in the sudden darkness, the sigh of the gasketed doors slowly closing. Muffled voices in the hallway faded to silence.

Cy counted to sixty twice before he crawled out of the gurney, and stretched with a groan. He found a rolling chair and sat in the dark. If that old fart professor returned, well, fuck it.

Sometime between five and ten minutes later the gasketed metal doors opened, and the lights flickered on. "Sorry about that," Ben said.

Cy rubbed his eyes in the light. "So that was Professor Baylor? He sounds like a mad scientist from an old horror movie."

Ben rotated a finger by his ear as he handed Cy his rucksack. "According to the rumor mill he talks to dead people."

"That's not so weird. That's, what, praying, right?"

Ben's laugh was hollow. "Not when he says they talk back."

Wednesday, October 2, 1974

Cy found the wide stairwell and second-floor hallway of the Fine Art Building (the FAB) mercifully empty, so he could run full tilt. He was seriously late to Professor Grakowski's oil painting studio class, so all the good easels and prime locations—including the one by the window where he had begun his current class painting—were taken. He was forced to use an easel on the side, farthest from the windows, with only the narrowest view of the model on the riser.

He hung his rucksack on the easel's crank handle, wormed his way across the crowded studio to the slat wall, and pulled out his canvas and palette. Making his way back with wet canvas and palette in either hand, Professor Grakowski called out from the other end of the big room, "Glad you could join us, Mr. Barnaby." Cy flashed him an embarrassed smile. He managed not to knock into anyone's easel the remaining steps back to his own. He set his canvas on the crossbar without even glancing at it, placed his palette on the top of his taboret table, then emptied his paints from the rucksack into the taboret's top drawer.

It took nearly a minute to get his brushes and paints ready, then about two seconds to confirm his painting in progress was still a piece of shit. The model, sitting on the stool with nothing on but a towel draped over one shoulder, was in the same location as last time, but from this new location it was a totally different pose, a totally new subject. He might as well start over. *Screw this,* he thought.

A throat cleared behind him. "You might just as well scrape that down and start again, Mr. Barnaby." Professor Grakowski leaned over his shoulder. "It's a totally different composition from here, don't you think?"

"I'll be fine," Cy said. He tapped his forehead with his forefinger. "Still got it up here."

"As you wish." Grakowski made his way to the center of the studio. "Ten more minutes till model break, people."

Cy hesitated. He looked at the model, then at his canvas. He looked at the model again, still hesitating. *Crap.* He grabbed his palette knife and began scraping off the still wet paint, down to the dry.

Thursday, October 3, 1974

Kate and Brenda looked up from their cereal when Cy entered the kitchen of their rooming house—Our House—trying to put his jacket on with one hand while holding his ruck-sack with the other.

Kate stopped him with an outstretched arm. "Hold your horses there, buddy-boy."

"You left your breakfast dishes in the sink again." Brenda pointed with her spoon.

"I've got a psych test. I'll do them later." Cy winced as he struggled with his jacket.

Kate noticed. "You okay?"

"I fell out of bed last night, hurt my shoulder."

"Anyone we know?"

"Very funny." He finally got his jacket on. "Leave your dishes for me and I'll do them too, when I get home. Promise. I really gotta go." Then he was out the door.

The two girls shared a look. "The real estate lady warned us about rooming with boys," Brenda said. She dropped her spoon in her bowl and pushed her chair back. "I'll wash?"

Kate did the same, with a sigh. "I'll dry."

"And if we somehow accidentally happen to drop anything of Cyrus's…?"

"Tough break," Kate said, grinning.

Friday, October 4, 1974

Whenever Ben returned from a stint in the medical college dissection rooms he took a shower, which suited Cy, Kate and Brenda just fine. Cy heard the shower stop, and after a minute or two, the bathroom door open. Then, "Hey."

Cy looked up from his American history textbook. Ben leaned against the doorjamb with nothing on but a towel, his curly dark hair still dripping. Behind him, through her open door across the landing, Kate raised her voice just short of a yell, "Can you please put some clothes on, Benjamin? I swear if that towel slips…."

Ben grinned over his shoulder. "You should be so lucky." He returned his attention to Cy. "I think I may have found a way out of our little dilemma."

Cy closed his textbook on a finger. "I'm listening."

"I heard Professor Baylor talking to Professor Finneran about needing an art student to do some work for him."

"What kind of work?"

"Drawing. Painting. Right up your alley. He's too old to do

it himself anymore." Ben held up a shaking hand. "He's got the shakes now. Know what I mean?"

"I don't get it. Drawing and painting what?"

"Medical stuff, I guess. Just like what you're already–" Ben dropped his voice to a whisper, "–*you know*. Only this time it would be *allowed*."

Drawing cadavers in secret, when Ben had his evening work-study job, was one thing. It was classic Da Vinci and Eakins, and extra cool because it sort of broke the rules. But under the supervision of a professor? Illustration on demand? Cy reopened his textbook. "How about this: I'll think about it."

"Fair enough."

"You didn't mention my name or anything, I hope."

"Oh hell no. They weren't talking to me; I just overheard them." Ben straightened, "I'm cool. We're cool." His towel slipped, and he grabbed at it.

"Benjamin," Kate growled.

"So close your door already!"

"I'm going to count to three. One…"

"Okay, okay!" Ben winked at Cy, then retreated to his room.

"You almost saw something special," Cy said across the landing.

Kate laughed. "With a microscope, maybe."

Ben, from his room, "Hey! I heard that!"

Saturday, October 5, 1974

"Hello! Cy? You down there?"

Cy paused, looking up. Kate. "Yep. Come on down."

He had claimed a corner, about a quarter of the basement, for a painting studio. The height to the floor beams was fine, the fluorescent lights adequate, and the heat from the grumbling old steam furnace kept it warm enough. Best of all, it was relatively private. The only time anyone ever came down was to do their laundry, and the washer and dryer were on the other side of the basement, beyond the furnace. Cy had been working on his new oil painting, his "big deal" painting, for over a month now. It was a Symbolist, photo-realistic full-length portrait of Caim, the Dark Angel. Caim stood knee-deep in poppies, with broadsword in hand, a tangled forest behind, its trees silhouetted against the last violet dregs of dusk…

Millais, Rossetti, Burne-Jones, all that Pre-Raphaelite Brotherhood crowd, would be proud.

Kate descended the creaking stairs and rounded the furnace, shaking her car keys. "Brenda and I are going food shopping. You need any – Wow." She stopped, open-mouthed, before the six-foot high painting. "Wow," she said again.

"So you hate it," he said.

"Are you kidding? I love it! The last time I looked it was just…"

"Underpainting."

"Whatever. It sure as heck wasn't *this*." She went up to it.

"Wet paint," Cy cautioned.

"I'm not going to touch it." She looked at him over her shoulder. "How come no face yet?"

"I can't decide. I want someone like Waterhouse's *Lady of Shalott*."

"I have that poster in my room."

"I know."

She looked at him again. "Everybody tells me I look just like her."

"I agree. You do."

"So?"

"So do you want to pose for it or not?"

She turned fully around. "Say that again?"

"Pose. For the face."

"Me?" Her expression mixed skeptical, embarrassed…and interested. "How hard would it be?"

"Not hard at all. Just a couple of sittings."

"So I can sit down?"

He nodded. "I need to get this done for the student show the end of November, before Thanksgiving, so we'd have to start, like, soon. You up for it?"

"Immortalized in a painting by the great Cyrus Barnaby?" Kate looked at the painting again. "Sure. It'll be a kick. Sign me up."

"Great. Cool. Thanks."

She turned back. "How long have you been waiting to ask me?"

"Since, well, when I first got the idea for the painting."

She shook her head, smiling. "You're too shy, Cyrus, you know that? Much too shy."

"Which is why I'm so popular, I guess." He shrugged. "Now I just need someone to translate the title into French. Since I'm so timid, though…"

"What are you calling it?"

"Are you ready? *Oh Dark Angel, Lost Among the Flowers of Oblivion.*"

"Hmm. Oblivion flowers. There are a couple of nuances, but French is lousy with nuances."

"Wait a minute, you know French?"

"And I bet you and all the other boys took Spanish in high school, right?" She raised a finger and wrote in the air: "Ô noir ange, perdu parmi les fleurs du néant."

He blinked. "I'm impressed. Sounds perfect."

"You could also go 'ô ange noir', or 'ô ange sombre'. You could also use 'l'oubli' or 'l'obscurité' instead of 'néante'."

"Nuances?"

"Yep. But I think the first translation might be best."

"First one it will be, then. Hey, thanks! 'Oh nowah ang…'"

She looked heavenward. "How about I write it down!"

Monday, October 8, 1974

Ben led Cy to the same dissection room as before. The closest drain table was the only one occupied. Ben folded the sheet back, exposing the lower half of a human leg. The knee had been opened up, skin pinned back. A rose vine tattoo traveled up from her ankle and disappeared under the skin fold. "What's left of poor Wilma," he said.

Cy pulled his sketchbook from his rucksack. "Fred, Wilma …I'm starting to recognize a theme here."

"We never know their real names."

"Honestly, I don't know how you do it."

Ben tapped his temple with his gloved finger. "It's really all up here. I swear you can get used to anything, if you have to."

Cy moved his stool close to the other side of the drain table, and looked at the exposed tendons and ligaments. "I'm going to enjoy this one." He opened his sketchbook to a new page, and selected a pencil.

Ten minutes later Ben straightened, bending his back with a groan. "Got a kink."

"You were in my way anyway," Cy said.

"Well excuse me." Ben looked at the drawing. "Not bad." He watched Cy draw. "I finally mentioned you to Professor Baylor, by the way."

"He's still looking for someone for that drawing job?"

"Yep. I think he tried somebody, but it didn't work out."

"What a shame." Cy erased an errant line. "I wish you hadn't done it."

"Done what?"

"Mentioned me to the guy."

"Hey, it was purely selfish on my part. If you start working for him, you won't have to sneak around anymore."

"You worried we might get caught again?"

"We've been lucky so far." Ben rubbed his nose with a clean knuckle. "I did find out what he wants drawn, anyway. Do you know what a meninges is?"

"Where you get meningitis?"

"Bingo. It's the tissue membrane that wraps around your brain and your spine, sort of a wall around the castle, protecting your goodies against infection. The meninges tissue that covers the brain is called a caul. Professor Baylor is all gaga over them."

"Takes all kinds, I guess. You said he talks to the cadavers?"

"Rumor mill update: he doesn't talk to them; he *reads* them."

Cy looked up from his drawing. "Reads them? What the hell does that mean?"

"He *sees* things in the meninges cauls. Like Jesus in a piece of toast, Elvis in a leaf, unicorn in a cloud, all that bullshit."

"So he wants to record the cauls in drawings? You'd think he'd get them photographed."

"You'd think, yeah. He's a crazy old guy. I think he's trying to add to a bunch of caul drawings and paintings he's collected, some of them pretty old. I know some of them are in folders in the medical library."

"Portfolios. Documents are in folders; art is in portfolios."

"Well excuse me Mr. Fine Arts Major."

Cy continued drawing. "I'm still not interested."

"I thought you might be curious to at least see them."

"Old pictures of dead tissue?"

"He sees words in the tissue. Messages from the *dead* for chrissakes." Ben imitated Dracula: "Eet might be coool."

"That's crazy." Cy erased another line. "And you, my friend, are weird."

Friday, October 11, 1974

"Don't move," Cy said.

Kate rolled her eyes. "You don't have to tell me that."

"Sorry. I forgot you're a hot-shit artist's model now." Cy continued painting. The furnace behind them rumbled. The pipes overhead began rattling, and the hanging cobwebs waved gently in the moving air.

"Let me know when you're doing my mouth," Kate said, "and I'll shut up."

"I need to get the secondary shadows down. Just the broad planes, nothing too specific."

"Cy."

"Sorry. You probably don't know what I'm talking about."

She pointed to herself. "Primary Education major here, remember?"

"Sorry."

"I swear, if you say you're sorry one more time I'm going to make a crazy face and start dancing here. Try painting *those* secondary shadows mister hot-shot artist's model artist."

Cy opened his mouth, then closed it, and they both laughed.

Someone walked into the dining room upstairs, then dragged something, briefly. A creak of floor boards, and then piano music penetrated down, that sonata Brenda was trying to learn.

"Oh God," Cy said. "I'm starting to get a little sick of that one."

"It's Beethoven. Cyrus," Kate said. "How can you be sick of Beethoven?"

The public phone in the first-floor hallway rang. The music stopped, and Brenda got it.

They heard her come to the basement door. She called down, "Cy? You down there? It's Ben."

"You sure got here fast," Ben said. He had a ratty *Rolling Stone* open before him on the morgue office desk, and a nearly empty bottle of Pepsi beside it.

Cy shrugged off his rucksack, then his jacket. "So what's the big secret?"

Ben finished the soda as he stood. "Did you bring your art stuff?"

Cy held up the rucksack. "You've got something for me to draw?"

"Oh yeah. Follow me."

Cy was growing used to the smell beyond the gasketed metal doors, but he still held his breath as they sealed shut behind them. Ben got the lights.

The four drain tables were empty. Ben pointed to the far

counter, to a lone metal pan covered with a pane of glass. "Baylor went absolutely apeshit over this today," he said, as they made their way to it. A haze of condensation covered the inside surface of the glass, but Cy could make out something large and flat. He dropped his rucksack to his feet. "One of those meninges cauls?"

"Just wait." Ben put on latex gloves, carefully lifted the glass, and slid it into the rack behind the pan. Then, slowly, he pulled the pan toward them. "This was Wilma's."

The pan held about an inch of clear fluid, formaldehyde, by the stink of it. The caul lay flat underneath, pinned to a blue neoprene pad. "It's big," Cy said. "Bigger than I imagined."

"Baylor harvested it himself, in Theater Two, all of us watching. I have to give him credit. He doesn't miss a trick, and he never leaves anything behind."

The meninges caul had been cut so its edges formed a series of pointed arches, like a Mercator map. "So this is the whole thing?"

"The entire sack, yeah. He trimmed it where it continued down the spinal cord. But look." Ben pointed. "What do you see?"

Cy bent over the pan, then pulled back, waving his hand in his face. "It's a little strong."

"Here." Ben went to a box down the counter and returned with a fresh gauze surgeon's mask. "This should help."

Cy put it on, took a sniff, and nodded. He bent over the pan again. "The capillaries are vivid."

"That's freshness for you. Plus it was just stained this afternoon."

Cy saw something. "Wait. Are those supposed to be letters?" They were regular patterns in the intricate capillary web, a mix of upper- and lower case. A–t–H. He saw more in the adjacent arch of tissue: e–r–H–e. And in the next: L–P–M. "Letters," he said. "I'm definitely seeing letters."

"I did too, after Baylor pointed them out. What do you think they say?"

"That first part has M–E–F, so: M–E–F–A–t–H–e–r–H–e–L–P–M. 'Me father help'."

"Good eye there, my artistic friend. Now look." Ben crowded in, pointing. "What about here, in the first section of tissue? I see e–L–P."

Then Cy did too.

Ben leaned back. "I don't think that's Emerson, Lake, and Palmer."

"No." Cy couldn't help but smile under his mask. "It's probably the last three letters of 'help'. Just like that last 'M' is probably the start of 'me.' 'Help me father help me.'"

"You really see that?"

"Don't you?"

Ben shook his head and shrugged at the same time. "I don't know what to think. I didn't see anything until Baylor showed us. It could be real letters and words, but it could also just be my brain doing it, connecting the dots on its own. Tigers in clouds, Jerry Garcia in a cracked sidewalk."

"Apophenia."

"Apple what?"

Cy pulled the surgeon mask down. "Apophenia." He tried to quote from memory: "The tendency to see or seek patterns or images in random visual information. Psych 102."

"You're actually awake in that class?"

"This isn't that, though. This is real. This is someone, some-how, from somewhere, trying to talk through living tissue."

Ben looked at him. "Like Wilma herself, maybe? Like we're all writing notes to ourselves in our heads? Literally?"

"Maybe. Who knows?"

"Well, shit. Suddenly I have an itch between my eyeballs."

Cy looked down at the caul. "Creepy stuff."

"Every time we cut someone up, we might find notes. That's off the scale of my creep-o-meter."

"So can I draw it now?"

"Knock yourself out." Ben pulled at his gloves. "I think I need some fresh air. I'm gonna make a security walk-around.

They are paying me, after all."

"You think Baylor may stop by?"

"Nah. He's probably nodding into his third highball by now." The gloves snapped, coming off. "Take your time. Document the crap out of it. Say hi to the ghosts for me."

"Ha ha," Cy said, reaching down for his rucksack.

Tuesday, October 15, 1974

The medical library in the main building of the Rackham School of Medicine was tiny compared to the campus library. Cy peeked through the tinted glass wall in the corridor. He counted a dozen shelf aisles, five tables, and one desk, with a plump, middle-aged librarian seated behind it. Behind her was a glass wall and another room with shelves, and that was it. Even the art library in the FAB was bigger.

"The portfolios are in the back room," Ben had told him. *"You have to ask for them, wear white gloves, all that kind of crap."*

"So they're old, then."

"Maybe. I've never seen them. Rare, anyway. That's why they're in the back."

No one looked up when he entered, not even the librarian when he went over and stood before her.

"Um, excuse me?"

She made a deliberate mark on the paper before her, sighed audibly, then gave him her attention. "Yes?"

"I was wondering if you—"

She put a finger to her lips.

In a whisper, he began again. "I was wondering if you could help me?"

A raised eyebrow was her only response.

"Professor Baylor—"

"*Doctor* Baylor."

"Right. Doctor Baylor. He has, well, someone told me he has some portfolios of drawings, in the back room. I was hoping

I could–"

"Those are in the *restricted* collection."

"Right. Well, I didn't want to check them out or anything. I only wanted to look at them."

She put her hand out, palm up. "ID?"

He dug his wallet out of his back pocket, pulled his identification card free and gave it to her.

She glanced at it, smiled a thin smile, and handed it back to him. "You're a student at Goddard."

"Well yeah, but–"

"Only Rackham students are allowed use of this library, and access to material in the restricted collection, and only then with a written request from faculty."

Cy stood there, his mouth open. "Um. So–"

"So I'm sorry. Have a good day." She returned her attention to the papers before her. Dismissing his skinny little Goddard School of Fine Art ass.

Wednesday, October 16, 1974

Cy woke abruptly from a sharp poke in his ribs. "Owww." He tumbled off his bed to the floor, landing on his hands and knees. *What the hell!* He got up, blinking in the darkness, feeling his side. *Was that a dream?* He felt his ribs, but there was no pain. *It must have been a dream.* Out his window a thin crescent moon peeked over the neighbor's roof. *Late. It must be past midnight at least.*

A dab of silver moonlight illuminated one of the old photos of his parents he had tacked up over his desk, the one taken on the boardwalk in Atlantic City, on their honeymoon. He stared at it for several seconds. They looked so happy.

The poke evoked a memory.

"You're so serious when you paint," his mom said, poking his ribs to make him laugh as she peered over his shoulder. She hugged him from behind. "You're my little serious artist, my little Serious Cyrus."

The sound of her voice, the memory, echoed clearly in his head. *Serious Cyrus.*

He draped his comforter around him, and went to the back window overlooking the kitchen roof and the parking lot. This late, the stars only had the sliver of moon for competition, and they crowded the sky. He made out Orion by the three stars of his belt, And Sirius, the bright star, to his left.

I really have to stop falling out of bed. He went back to bed, felt his ribs again, *weird, weird dream*, rolled himself in the comforter, and tried to fall back to sleep.

Outside, the stars wheeled silently, imperceptibly, across the sky.

Thursday, October 17, 1974

Cy brought a sandwich into the living room, and took possession of the rear couch. "Still nothing?"

Ben kicked the side of the television console. "I think we need more tin foil for the antenna."

"Here." Cy put his plate down. "Let me try."

He moved the antenna rabbit ears slowly, his eyes on the snowy screen. "I tried to get a look at those portfolios of Professor Baylor's, by the way."

"Oh yeah? What did you think?"

"No soap. The wicked witch at the desk wouldn't let me at them."

"She can be a pain in the ass when she wants to. Maybe try at night, when the TAs and grad students have shifts."

"Maybe." Cy saw the ghost of images in the white noise static.

"So what about, you know, the job thing?"

Cy continued moving the antenna. "I have an appointment with Baylor tomorrow."

"Seriously?"

"I figure it might be fun." The snow cleared somewhat, and

the bridge of the USS Enterprise came into focus. "There you go." Cy went back to his sandwich. "I like this episode."

Ben dove onto the other sofa. "Me too."

Brenda wandered in. "What's on? Ooh! I love this one." She took a seat next to Cy, and sniffed. "Ham?"

"And swiss." He handed her the other half of his sandwich.

She kissed his cheek. "You were always my favorite, Cyrus."

"Feed them sandwiches," Ben grumbled, across the room. "Check."

"You're learning," Brenda said, her mouth full.

Friday, October 18, 1974

The main building of the Rackham School of Medicine—and most of the rest of the original buildings crowding the old campus quad—reminded Cy of his junior high school: built during the Depression, skintled brick facades, form-cast concrete pillars, lintels and sills, marble steps, and huge nine-over-nine paned windows whose frames were eternally in need of a good scrape and repainting. Inside, the air was heavy with old chalk, piney cleaners, and fifty years of floor wax and cigarette smoke.

Mirror-image staircases flanked the wide entry hall. Cy chose the left one, and went up to Room 214. This was serious professor-office territory, half the doors open, quiet conversations spilling out, pleadings, cajolings, and pontifications. Professor Baylor's office was at the end, the last one on the left, beside the high Palladian window. Age-darkened oak-framed two expanses of translucent, pebbled glass on either side of the closed door. Bells tolled, soft with distance. Cy looked out the window to the clock tower of the library across campus; twelve noon on the dot. The murmurings of conversation along the hall made him lean close, listening for sounds in Baylor's office. Finally, he knocked.

"Come."

He entered, taking in a confusion of filing cabinets, heavy

oak tables, bookcases with stacked and spilled piles of papers, books and binders, and a stuffed, dusty chimpanzee on an equally dusty iron stand, staring at him with bright black marble eyes.

"Yes? What is it?"

Cy broke eye contact with the chimp. Professor Baylor–short, plump, balding, with crazy sideburns that almost touched at his chin, and a pair of large, thick glasses perched high on the long slope of his forehead–sat behind a huge, littered desk in the center of the room. A stuffed turkey buzzard with wings outstretched–*like the big Wyeth tempera*, Cy thought; *like* Soaring –turned slowly on a braided cable high above him, caught in bars of sunlight. "Yes?" the professor said again, with a note of obvious impatience.

"I'm Cyrus Barnaby, sir. Benjamin Roth–"

"Ah. I recall. You're the art student. The rogue *draftsman*." The professor dropped his glasses to his nose with a quick nod of his head. "Young Roth sings your praises, Mr. Barnaby."

Cy gave an embarrassed shrug.

"So you are the secret visitor, sneaking in to draw the cadavers?"

"I– Uh–"

Baylor smiled. "Mr. Roth thinks there are secrets, eh? From me?"

"Well…"

Baylor motioned impatiently. "Did you bring the painting? The watercolor of the tissue sample?"

Cy fumbled with his rucksack straps, pulled out his sketchbook, extracted the little painting of the caul, and handed it across.

Baylor gave it his full attention, his eyes darting. Then he grunted, and looked up. "I questioned Mr. Roth when he said you were capable of drawing anything placed before you, with accuracy."

"As long as it's there in front of me, I can draw it, sure."

"Good." Baylor put the watercolor aside. "Come. Here."

He indicated a chair, piled with books, beside his desk. He waved his hand at the books. "Put them on the floor."

Cy did so, wiped the outline of dust off the seat, and sat.

"So. Show me what else you have done."

Cy gave him the sketchbook.

The professor opened it with a satisfied chuckle, and began turning pages rapidly, moving from one image to the next. Cy wished he would go slower, but kept his mouth shut. Finally, the old man paused. "So you have indeed been drawing our cadavers. That is plain."

"Yes sir."

"A young Leonardo, eh?"

"I wish."

"This," Baylor pointed, "must be Fred. His arthritis is unmistakable." He chuckled again, and slapped the sketchbook shut. "So. Mr. Roth was correct. You can draw and paint."

Cy said nothing, but nodded once.

"Now." The professor rummaged in the book and journal piles before him, and extracted an old brick-colored portfolio case. "Now I will show *you* something. Something that only recently came into my possession." He worried at the ribbon knot with fumbling fingers. Cy wanted to take it from him and do it himself, *my God*, but the old man finally got it loose, and opened the cover leaves. A dozen or so ink and wash drawings were revealed.

"Old work, sir?"

"Yes indeed. Old in fact, but still new to me. They were found this past summer in an antiquarian bookshop in England." Baylor glanced up, blinking behind his glasses, "East Anglia. Norwich. Near the university there." He began spreading the drawings out, side by side, with care. "Most are dated. This first row is from the eighteenth century, the rest are early nineteenth, though."

Cy moved his chair closer. "They're nice." Patterns, like lacework, in pinks, blues and browns. "Medical illustrations?"

Baylor nodded. "They are all representations in watercolor

and ink of human tissue."

Was this anything like the portfolios squirreled away in the restricted collection of the medical library downstairs? Cy pointed to the one nearest to him. "May I?"

"Er…yes, by all means."

The paper was thick and stiff, so it was easy to pick it up by its edges. Cy tilted it toward the window. The natural light caught and silvered the brown oxide of the iron in the ink. "This is a caul?"

"A portion of a meninges caul, yes."

"The illustrator did the washes first, over a graphite pencil sketch, then did the ink lines on top."

"Indeed."

"The ink drawing is not comprehensive, though, not complete." Cy looked up. "I've seen the real thing, so I can tell that not all the capillaries were inked in."

"Indeed," Baylor said again. "Only the major ones were included. Primary through tertiary."

"So this is writing?" Cy tried to catch the old man's eyes. "These are words, somehow? Real words?"

Baylor visibly stiffened. "That is not a discussion we will be having, young man."

"But–"

The professor took the watercolor drawing from him, and began gathering the others. "Whatever conversation you may have had with our Mr. Roth, whatever you may have heard on that subject, please…" he raised his hand briefly, "I have no interest in pursuing. Yes?"

"Sure. Yes sir. Whatever you say."

Baylor looked at him, slowly tapping a finger. Then he came to a decision. "My requirement is thus: someone who can draw and paint like this. And you can. I require someone who is available when I need them, to work while the tissue is fresh."

"I can't skip classes."

"Of course not. Flexibility is all I require. So. Five dollars an hour, cash, from me. A personal contract, not a work-study.

Enough? Enough. Agreed? Agreed. You will work here, in my office." He turned to point behind him. "That table there by the windows affords a generous north light. I will give you funds for all materials you might need, but everything stays here. You take nothing away. So. Do you want the job?"

A telephone rang, somewhere in the room.

"Yes. Yes sir," Cy said, over it.

Baylor lifted a pile of paperback journals, then a thick book, and picked up the phone receiver he found underneath. He turned in his swivel chair, held a finger up for Cy's benefit, and cradled the crusty old receiver against his cheek. "Yes? Yes? Newcombe! Yes, I was just—" He held his finger up again, ragged fingernail, yellow acid stairs. "Absolutely! Yes, I agree …yes, but I think—"

Cy got to his feet, shoved his sketchbook into his rucksack, and slung it over his shoulder. He used his own finger to point toward the door.

Baylor nodded. "One moment, please, John." He covered the mouthpiece. "Next Thursday, we will have a fresh caul, I believe. Five o'clock, yes? You will be here? Here," and he pulled a twenty-dollar bill from his vest pocket, "this should cover materials to begin, yes?"

Cy took the money. "Um, one more thing? Could I get a note from you to the medical library, so I can get access to the restricted collection?"

Baylor's sudden grin was nicotine and coffee-stained. "Those old things?" He uncovered the phone to wave his hand. "Tomorrow. Check my box in the office downstairs." He waved his hand one more time, dismissing Cy, and returned to his telephone caller.

Saturday, October 19, 1974

For some reason, maybe so he could say he had actually done it, Cy listened to all four sides of the latest YES album, even Side Three, which was godawful. He used his headphones to spare Kate, who preferred her Joni Mitchell and Bonnie Raitt, and Brenda the music major, who insisted on all that classical crap. Cy's tastes varied a bit: from James Taylor, Neil Young, Beatles, Al Stewart, Poco, to King Crimson, Pink Floyd, ELP ...and YES, of course. Even Side Three of *Tales From Topographic Oceans*.

When he finally pulled his headphones off, the clock radio read 11:25. He yawned. The rest of the house was quiet. Saturday night at Our House. When he went to pee, everyone's doors were shut. Brenda's had a light showing under hers, but the other two were dark. Saturday night at Our House indeed. Returning to his room, he locked his door, made sure the stereo was turned off, then took off his jeans, socks and sweater and slid under his comforter. Outside, a breeze moaned softly past his windows, tossing tree shadows across the ceiling. He turned off the lamp beside his bed, flopped onto his back, and watched the leaf shadows dance.

Then he heard, faintly, the sound of someone crying. Someone weeping.

He didn't move.

Was it Brenda? Kate?

He got out of bed, and went first to the wall he shared with Brenda, then to his door. No. Not them. The weeping, the quiet sobbing, was from somewhere else, distinct and clear, but farther away. From somewhere else. He returned to bed, and listened until it slowly faded to silence.

He gathered his comforter around him.

Silence. A silence that stretched....

Next door, through the wall, he heard a chair scrape across the floor. He went into the hall, and saw the sliver of light under Brenda's door was still there. He knocked, heard another chair scrape, and Brenda opened her door. She was in pj's and robe, her wavy red hair loose about her shoulders. "Cyrus," her voice barely above a whisper. "I was trying to be quiet. What's up?"

"Did you hear anything, just before?"

"What do you mean?"

"A few minutes ago, did you hear anything? Like someone crying?"

"No, just the wind, just a little. Crying? Kate?"

Cy shook his head. "She's asleep. So's Ben."

"Well it wasn't me. I'm burning the midnight oil to get this Lit paper done. It's due Tuesday. Henry James? Talk about a snooze…" She stopped, her expression puzzled. "You're serious? You heard someone crying?"

"Nah." He wiped his mouth. "I must have been dreaming."

"Maybe someone outside?"

He shook his head. "You would have heard it too."

"Yeah." She peered at him over her glasses. "You okay?"

"I'm fine." He looked past her. "Hey, I hear Henry James calling."

"That rat bastard." She grinned. "I'll be quiet. Go back to sleep." Her door closed with a quiet click.

Wednesday, October 23, 1974

Cy found Ben in the Capen Hall concourse, seated cross-legged on a low retaining wall in the shadow of the Student Union.

"You're late," Ben said, waving his apple. "I'm already at dessert."

"There was a line."

"Well you gotta–" Ben looked at the paper plate Cy held. "What the hell is that?"

Cy sat, cradling the plate in his lap. "It's a black bean and cheddar cheese burrito."

"It looks like a big fat turd."

"Gee, thanks." Cy fanned his hand over it.

"The snack bar is selling Mexican food now?"

"They got that new microwave oven thing."

Ben wiggled his fingers at the plate. "A radioactive Mexican egg roll. Sounds delicious." He tossed his apple core into the bushes behind him, and slid off the wall to his feet. When he swung his pack over his shoulder he nearly clipped two girls walking by.

"Hey!" The closest one turned, her long hair fanning out, "Watch it asshole!"

Ben grinned at her. "At least you know my name."

She smiled back, but gave him the finger anyway.

"You bring out the best in people, Benjamin," Cy said.

"Yeah, I'm famous for that." Ben slipped his other arm through the remaining strap, settling the pack. "Almost forgot: I saw your secret crush before."

Cy lifted the burrito, then dropped it. *Still way too hot.* "What secret crush?"

"That brunette, the art student, the one who's in black all the time, with the big bazongas and all the makeup."

Betsy Moone. "She's not my secret crush. I've never even talked to her."

"Tell that to your boner every time you see her walk by. Anyway, she was over the other side of Coykendall, near the library, setting up for some kind of show."

"Probably a performance piece. Conceptual Art Bullshit 101." Cy took a bite of the burrito. "Oh boy! Hot!" He waved his hand in front of his open mouth.

"Radiation, like I said. You'll probably have three-eyed children now."

Cy swallowed, and regarded his lunch. *Seventy-five cents for this?*

"She was drawing a crowd, whatever she's doing. Anyway. Enjoy your toxic waste dump there. Catch you later." Ben stepped into the concourse flow.

The next bite of the burrito was cold, and tasted like cardboard. *Enough.* Cy folded the plate over it, and tossed it in the nearest bin. Coykendall had a pass-through corridor, so he took it, emerging into the Excelsior concourse. The sizable crowd of students showed him where to go. Rather than elbow his way through, he climbed onto the opposite retaining wall, and gained a clear view over everyone's head.

Betsy Moone, wearing her signature black silk and leather, stood in a flat, empty planting bed adjacent to the Sojourner Truth Library. Her eye-makeup today was violet, her lipstick so dark it was almost black against her ivory skin. Even from here he could see her nipples straining against her silk blouse. *She must be freezing her tight little ass off. Jesus.* She had unrolled a large piece of brown Kraft paper, at least four or five feet of it, in the dirt before her.

A scruffy student in a worn Army coat and wooly scarf climbed to stand next to him. "Everybody says she's gonna strip," he said.

Cy glanced at him. "In this cold?"

"She's already not wearing a coat. Plus she did it before."

"You're kidding."

"No. Sincerely. I heard." The student wiped his nose with a knuckle. "Crazy art student."

"I'm an art student."

"Yeah, well, sorry man. She's totally stacked anyway."

"Can't argue that one." *Is she looking at me? Yeah.* Betsy had seen and recognized him and she gave him a small, secret smile.

"Hey," the student beside him wiped his nose again, "she's smiling at me."

Cy let it go.

Betsy spread her arms, and curtsied to the crowd, to loud clapping and a few whistles. She reached into her vest, under the swell of her left breast, and brought out a small plastic bottle containing a pale yellow liquid. *Jesus, is she kidding?*

Cy heard several hoots and whistles from the crowd of students. Someone yelled, "Show us, Mama!"

Betsy grinned at the source, then put a finger to her lips: shhhh. She popped off the plastic cap with a crimson thumbnail. Holding the bottle at arm's length, she began pouring the contents in a thin stream, onto the Kraft paper. The yellow liquid steamed in the air. *Piss? Is it really her piss?* When the bottle was empty, she raised it up, then tossed it into the crowd.

"She wrote something!"

"What's it say?"

The crowd surged up against the retaining wall.

"It says 'pussy'!"

"No, 'piss on me.'"

Betsy stood with legs apart, hands on hips, like some Marvel Comics superhero. She yelled at the crowd, "Piss on me!" Then, louder, "Come on! Who's got the balls? Piss on me!"

Laughter ran through the crowd, and then someone said, "You asked for it bitch!" and even from across the concourse, and through the confused sounds of the crowd, Cy heard a zipper come down.

Movement, then, and someone tall, a professor…Cy drew a blank for a second…Professor Frederick, from the art college, Mr. "Conceptual Art" himself, dropped a hand on the shoulder of the student with his fly open. The student looked up, angry, and Frederick increased his grip. "She's a young lady," he said, "and an artist. Apologize."

The student squirmed, "Hey man! What the hell?"

Frederick refused to release him. "Apologize."

"Okay! Hey, sorry, okay? Shit, she *asked* us to!"

Frederick smiled the same time Cy did. "Now zip up," Frederick said.

The student beside Cy said, "Was he really gonna do it? Piss on her?"

Performance art. The Phenomenological Consideration of Being. Jesus Christ. "Stranger things have happened," Cy said. "Crazy art students after all, right?"

The sun had set beyond the library's first floor window wall by the time Cy surfaced from his second draft of the Psych paper he needed to finish. He looked at his Timex. "Crap." The student sharing the long library table looked up, smiled briefly, then returned to her work.

His first stop was Professor Baylor's office. He wasn't expecting the professor to be there—their appointment wasn't until tomorrow—but what the hell. The cavernous second-floor hall was empty, and the professor's door, as expected, was locked. Inside, a random spear of sunlight through the drawn blinds caught one of the glass eyes of the stuffed chimp, causing it to sparkle like a jewel in the shadows. No one home. No one alive, anyway.

His next stop was the faculty office on the first floor, where the lone work-study student on duty welcomed the opportunity to rummage through Professor Baylor's box to find the envelope with Cy's name scrawled on it. "This what you're looking for?"

His final stop was the medical library. That door was also locked, but a paper sign taped to it said the library would re-open at six thirty. *Cool.* He took off his coat, made a cushion out of it, and sat cross-legged in the hallway with his rucksack in his lap.

The graduate student who eventually arrived—slender, freckles across her nose, curly auburn hair down past her shoulders—jingled her set of keys, and smiled down at Cy. "Have you been waiting long?"

He smiled back as he got up. "I was early, no big deal."

"Dedication!" She unlocked and opened the door.

Cy picked up and shook out his coat, "Jury's still out on that."

She turned on the lights, and tossed her pocketbook into the swivel chair behind the big desk. "You're not a med student."

"It's that obvious?"

She pointed to his paint splattered jeans. "Unless you're double-majoring. Can I help you find what you're looking for?"

He told her.

She whistled. "Prof Baylor actually wrote you a note?"

He produced it. She read it with wide eyes. "Well, well, well. Now it starts to make sense." She nodded to the glass-partitioned section of the library behind the desk. "They're back there." She jingled her keyring again. "We need another key. You want all of them?"

"How many are there?"

"Three, I think."

"Yeah. All three, then."

"Have a seat. I'll bring them out."

The three portfolio cases she placed in front of him were leather-bound, with blank covers. Their cloth hinges and ribbon ties were violet satin. Two of the portfolios were visibly old, their bindings and ribbons faded and water-stained, the leather foxed and worn at the edges and corners. The third portfolio, the one on top, looked new by comparison. The grad student brushed her hand across its cover. "Be nice if someone dusted back there."

"No problem. It's fine. Thanks." Cy pulled the portfolios toward him.

"You'll need these." She offered him a pair of white cotton gloves.

"Cool," he said, taking them.

Smiling again, she retreated back to her desk.

He donned the gloves, then put the top case aside, and chose one of the old ones. The ribbon was tied in a simple bow, and opened with ease. The binding endpapers were marbled in blue, pink and maroon. The smell of the old oil-based ink was unmistakable. The contents of the portfolio were leaves of linen watercolor paper, thick handmade stock, expensive stuff, *wonderful* stuff, separated by sheets of glassine. The first page held only a name: "Thomas Fettes Christie, MD, PhD" in fancy calligraphic lettering, and a date: 1889. He did the math on his fingers: 85 years old, probably 86. He turned the page. Both sides of the spread, facing and verso, contained a handwritten index: names, dates, addresses, and short notes, all in ordered, blue-lined columns. Page numbers too, so maybe this was a table of contents as well. He looked down the column of names. Nearly all were male, all with English, Scottish or Dutch surnames, with a few Irish thrown in. Salts of the earth, probably, all of them.

All long dead. All autopsied, dissected, and recorded. Here.

Cy turned the page and the glassine sheet, and his breath caught in his throat.

"You okay over there?"

Cy looked up. The desk lamp cast the grad student's eyes in shadow. "Yeah," he said, "I'm fine."

She grinned. "Just checking."

The facing page was a watercolor, delicately drawn and colored, of a meninges caul. Dr. Christie had even painted in the pins that drew the tissue taut. Cy reached down to his rucksack and pulled out his sketchbook, then his rubber-banded collection of pencils. He found the first blank page in the sketchbook and began drawing, carefully copying every blood vessel, every spidery capillary that the doctor had documented so many years ago. When he was done he compared the two, original watercolor and his pencil copy, side by side. Not bad. But no letters, no words, no message emerged from the patterns. It was only a caul. He turned the page in the portfolio, and almost laughed out loud. There, on the verso side of the watercolor, Christie had scribbled in pencil, "Only a caul."

Cy moved the next glassine sheet aside to reveal the next image. Another caul, of course, much like the first one. Before doing anything else, he checked the verso side: "Only a caul" had been written here as well.

The next caul watercolor, the same.

The fourth, however, made him pause. He looked closely, following the blood vessel patterns. *Something...*

He turned the page over. There, in block printed letters: "LOST MY WAY."

"Holy shit," he whispered.

Across the room, the grad student looked up as a student entered and flashed their ID.

He turned back to the caul watercolor, and carefully, in pencil, copied it into his sketchbook.

Checking the index pages, he found a narrow column with a scattering of "X"s in red ink. This watercolor had a corresponding "X" in the index. *Ah-hah!*

In the next three hours, he copied eight more watercolors and located five more from the portfolio, all with red "X"s, all with messages in the blood vessel patterns.

The messages were simple and straightforward, some mixing capitals with lower-case letters:

"IT IS DARK"

"I am COLD"

"WHERE ARE YOU"

"DANIEL came to ME"

"LORD hear my"

"NO COLOURS NO COLOURS"

"HE is heer"

"Who is this"

"I AM LOSTT"

And a few that made no sense at all:

"baecern beO IC"

"SE angnesse forjigeseeft"

"deos MIN eordbyrgen"

And one he couldn't stop coming back to:

"I LOVE THOU LOVE Where ART THOU"

He finally had to stop. He was starting to get sloppy, and this work could not be that; it had to be accurate; it had to be perfect.

He brought the three portfolios and gloves up to the grad student. "I have to come back another time to finish."

She took them from him. "You saw the dust. They're not going anywhere." She held up the gloves. "You say you're planning on coming back?"

"Yeah."

"Then keep these." She handed the gloves back.

"You've been a big help."

She smiled at him. "I appreciated the company."

Saturday, October 26, 1974

Usually, Cy only remembered those dreams he had just

before waking in the morning. This time, though, the dream he remembered came in the dead of night:

He was making out with some girl, on some couch, in some darkened room, and when he managed to work his free hand under her sweater, and then her well-tucked-in shirt, he knew it was the graduate student with the freckles and long curly hair. He could smell her perfume when he nuzzled her neck, and the citrus scent of her shampoo. Music was playing, but he didn't recognize the band. It filled the gaps, though, and felt almost as perfect as her caresses and urgent kisses.

Gotta go for third base, right? That thought appeared utterly rational, totally possible. She seemed so *yielding*... So he dipped his hand into her jeans, slipping behind the elastic of her panties, marveling at the smoothness of her skin, at the warmth, at the—

SLAP!

He woke up, still feeling the sting of the dream slap on his cheek.

What time is it, anyway? He looked at the faintly glowing numbers of his clock radio: 12:51.

His cheek still stung. *Did I scratch myself?* He turned on the nightstand lamp, looked at himself in the narrow mirror on his closet door, and his mouth hung open. His cheek had a handprint across it in vivid pink, a real slap, *the* slap.

Holy shit. He looked around his room, his eyes bright and wide. The silence was like a fog, surrounding him. His door was closed. No one else was in the room.

He found himself looking at the far corner, the one where the north and west walls met, looking at the shadows there. The high dresser cast one shadow, the pumpkin crate holding his records cast another. But it was the *other* shadow, the *third* one, he couldn't figure out. The corner was no more than eight feet away, and even with only the one lamp lit, it was plain to see. Dresser and crate, that was all. *So what's making the third shadow?*

He flung the comforter aside, got up and went over. He crouched to put his hand out, touching first one wall, then the other. When he ran his fingers across the floorboards he left faint tracks in the otherwise undisturbed dust. He rocked back on his heels. From here, there was no third shadow.

He looked behind him, then to the closet door, then everywhere else. *Could it be?* He brought his hand to his cheek, looking out into the darkness.

He returned to bed, finally, switched off the lamp, and got back under the comforter. He turned on his side so he could see the corner, lit now only with the faint blue glow from the streetlights outside. The faint shadows from before were lost in the general darkness. The furnace came on, a quiet grumbling, and after a minute his radiator began to ping, and then hiss. He shivered, pulled the comforter up to his chin, and forced his eyes to close. "Goodnight," he whispered.

Thursday, October 31, 1974

Cy chose to spend Halloween afternoon sitting on an old blanket on the tin-roofed slope of the front porch. The biggest limbs of the two ancient buttonwood trees arched overhead, and he found himself dodging the occasional big, twirling leaf. Below, on the porch, Kate, Brenda, and Chloe, a friend of Brenda's from the Music School, were the Three Witches, handing out candy to the trick-or-treaters.

"Some help here?"

Cy took the six-pack from Ben, and gave him room to clamber awkwardly out the front bathroom window. "Professional Dance's loss is Medicine's gain," Cy said.

"And screw you too. So we're sitting on the porch roof for Halloween?"

"On a blanket, and the beer's free. You got a problem?"

"Hell no. Give me one."

Cy pulled a can free and handed it over, then took one for himself. Below, the witches shrieked and cackled, and the costumed kids shrieked back, their feet like stampeding cattle on the porch steps and floorboards. "Don't tell me." He pointed down. "Green makeup? Wigs? Cone hats with comets and stars on them?"

"And cheap black graduation robes, I think. Kate's idea. They even scared the shit out of me."

Cy sipped his beer. "I miss Halloween."

"One of my top holidays," Ben said, nodding.

"I just wish I didn't have to give this one up."

"You could still do something...like cut holes in a sheet, scrunch down, talk in a falsetto like this: 'Trick or treat please!'"

Cy picked up a big flat leaf and frisbee'd it off to the root-rumpled sidewalk below.

Across the street a trail of monsters, princesses, cowboys and batgirls walked the length of the lumberyard sidewalk to the big Victorian next door. Cy counted ten carved and lighted pumpkins on their porch, the railings draped in fake spider webs, with two tall harvest shocks of straw framing the front door. "I wonder what they're giving out?"

"Big candy bars, I bet. Just like us. Kate went around with a collection, remember?"

"And I was happy to contribute. No bullshit candy corn at Our House."

Ben belched. "Fuck no." He drained his can, and tossed it back, through the open window.

"Hey," Cy said, "that's Kate and Brenda's bathroom."

"Better than hitting a little Charlie's Angel on the head anyway." Ben pulled another beer free, popped it, and took a healthy slug. "This is shit beer."

Cy acknowledged the point with a nod.

"Not another one for you?"

"Baylor said he'd have another caul for me to paint. He wants me there by five."

Ben belched. "Well that's not happening."

"What do you mean?"

"The cadaver delivery for today was postponed."

"Seriously?"

"As a corpse. Some mixup at the county morgue in Poughkeepsie." Ben reached over, pulled a can free, and handed it to him. "No painting for you today, my macabre artistic friend, so drink up."

A cold breeze swept the roof, rattling the remaining leaves in the buttonwoods, and sending some of those on the roof sailing off into space. Below, the witches cackled, and the children squealed.

Ben raised his can. "To shit beer and misplaced cadavers."

They tapped cans, chugged them, then threw the empties over their shoulders, through the window. The cans clattered across the tile floor.

Kate's voice drifted up: "You two are cleaning our bathroom, you know!"

Ben yelled at the blanket between his knees, "We love you Kate!" Then he rolled his eyes at Cy and whispered, "Jesus!"

Friday, March 25, 1960

He remembered getting visitors in the hospital, and every time he thought it would be his parents. But it never was.

His Aunt Carol and Uncle Fred came often, always with a toy that he wasn't allowed to play with yet, but had to be set aside, for later.

"It's going to be okay." Aunt Carol said, over and over, patting his hand, the one not punctured with catheters. "It's going to be fine. You'll be fine, good as new. You'll see."

But he remembered thinking: *No, I won't. I won't, ever.*

2

Friday, November 1, 1974

The graduate student with the curly auburn hair told him she had three evening shifts in the medical library: six thirty to ten on Mondays, Wednesdays, and Fridays. When Cy arrived at seven—after making sure the daytime librarian had gone home to bake little children into pies—he saw that the grad student had already taken out the three portfolios for him.

"You're a mind reader," he whispered, smiling.

She returned the smile as she handed them over. "You wanted all three again, right?"

"Oh yeah."

"You still have the gloves?"

He pulled them out of his coat pocket. "I owe you."

"A beer at the Union after we close would be nice."

What? He visibly hesitated. *Really?*

She looked at him with an amused smile.

Cyrus, he thought, *you haven't a clue.* "Um, sure, sounds good," he said, then retreated to an open table.

He wasn't here to copy patterns this time. That took too long. He was here solely for the words. He donned his gloves, and opened the oldest portfolio, another stack of watercolors on thick, rich stock, with sheets of glassine between them. Someone had stamped HMRMC EDINBURGH on the inside front cover, in red ink. A name was written carelessly below it, in black ink: "Alistair MacFee." Nothing else; no title, no attribution. Maybe MacFee had been a student at the Royal Medical College, drafted like him for his artistic talents.

This portfolio had no index, no information at all in front, and in particular, no column of red "X"s. *Damn.* Maybe he would have to copy the watercolors after all.

He spread the top three paintings on the table. *Yikes.* Whatever talents Alistair MacFee may have possessed, painting had not been one of them.

He restacked the watercolors in order, then opened his notebook and tested the point on his pencil. Then he gave his full attention to the watercolor on top, the pale rose washes of tissue, the dark maroon spider web of capillaries, and relaxed his eyes…

The Dragon's Den snack bar at the Student Union was doing a brisk business, but Cy and the graduate student managed to get two beers and an empty table without spilling anything.

"So," Cy said, hands around his plastic cup.

The graduate student pointed a long finger, its nail painted cream, at her chest. "Gloria."

"So, Gloria. You're a med student?"

"Nope. Forensic Chemistry." She took a sip of her beer.

"You mean, like, crime scenes and dead bodies?"

"Not really. Police usually have crime scene teams of actual policemen, and medical examiners deal with the bodies. I will be the one in the lab, processing the evidence they give me."

"So that's why—"

"Why I knew about the portfolios? Partly. Plus I had heard the stories. I was curious." She put her beer down and leaned forward. "So why are you interested? For the painting part? Because you're an art major?"

He saw her expression and grinned. "I know: a BFA and fifty cents will get me an all-day ride on the subway."

She laughed. "Are you any good?"

He liked that she knew nothing about him. "I'm still learning," he said.

"I'd love to see your work."

He looked at her, then ducked his head.

"I mean," she said, reading him, "do you have anything in the upcoming student show?"

"Yeah. I got one in."

"Well good for you. I'll be sure to look for it." She took another sip of her beer. "So you still haven't said why you're so interested in those portfolios. And don't tell me you're just curious too."

He decided to be cautious. "I'm just studying the art, like you said."

"Oh come *on*." She gave him a raspberry, her eyes doing a little roll. "Wasn't that note from Dr. Baylor? We both know it's those stories. You think you're the first? Why do you think we keep them locked up?" She pointed to the rucksack at his feet. "Show me what you're doing."

"You really want to see?"

"I'm curious too, remember?" She pointed again. "Show me."

"Hey Glo."

They both looked up.

A short, thin, twenty-something with a three-day growth of beard and spiky, unkempt brown hair, grinned down at her with a mouth full of bad teeth, as though Cy wasn't there at all. "Tutoring high school kids now?"

Gloria's voice was just north of a growl, "Get lost, Howard."

Howard's sneer was enough for Cy, and he began getting up.

Gloria put her arm out to stop him. "No, please, don't. Howard is leaving."

Howard's sneer remained. "Seriously? You're blowing *me* off?"

Now Cy did get up, finally getting Howard's attention. Cy was only a little over five nine, but he was still taller than this asshole. "Seriously," he said. "She said leave. Like right now."

"Now…boys…."

Howard took a step back. "Like I said. High school."

Cy matched Howard's backward step with a forward step of his own.

Howard continued his retreat, knocking into first one person, then another. Then he was lost in the assembling crowd.

Cy sat back down to a scattering of applause. "That was weird."

Gloria sighed. "That's Howard."

"You should get new friends."

"I'm trying." She patted his hand. "Or haven't you noticed."

"So what is he, another forensic chemistry grad student?"

"No, thank God. Anyway." She nodded to his rucksack. "You were about to show me."

"I was?"

She gave him a warning look.

He produced his sketchbook, flipped through it briefly, then pushed it across the table, careful of the beer cups. "Here are two recent ones."

She looked at the pencil sketches closely, totally absorbed. "These aren't in the portfolios."

"I thought you wanted to see new ones."

She looked up. "New like Rackham morgue cadaver new?"

He nodded. "These are sketches of the watercolors. The professor's got those."

"You're doing them for him?"

Cy put his hand out, parallel to the table. "He's old, has the shakes, can't do it himself any more. Nothing official; he's paying me under the table."

"So you're his hired gun? The hot-shit painting major?"

"Hey," he said, "watch it."

"I'm smiling, jeez, so sensitive!"

"I got the impression he doesn't trust photography. Like it misses stuff."

"I agree." She studied the sketches again. "Do these say anything?"

"The one on your left says 'where are they.'" He used his

finger to trace the capillaries. "See? 'W–H–E–R–E.'"

"Oh my God." She shivered. "*I do*." Cy saw a trace of new alarm in her eyes. "I never really saw it until now. You're sure you didn't…"

"I didn't make it up," he said.

She traced with her own finger. "I really see it. It's not just an asterism."

"Asterism?"

"A shape you see in nature that looks like something else. Like in stars, like the Big Dipper."

"I thought the Big Dipper was a constellation."

"Oh yeah, you're an art major all right. The Big Dipper is an asterism *in* a constellation, Ursa Major."

"So you mean like the belt and sword in Orion?"

"There you go. You're not so hopeless after all." She turned the page to two more caul sketches.

"Sketches of watercolors again," Cy said.

She nodded. "These I recognize. From the second portfolio. Is there anything here?"

"The one on the right. But it's not in English." Cy grabbed a notebook from his rucksack, flipped through it to a dog-eared page. "I wrote them out."

Gloria took it from him. "B–a–e–c–e–r–n–space–b–e–O–space–I–C. Upper- and lower-case; interesting."

"There's another one even crazier, from the same portfolio." Cy reached across to flip the page.

Gloria read it aloud: "S–E–space–a–n–g–n–e–s–s–e–space–f–o–r–j–i–g–e–s–e–e–f–t." She took a long moment. "That's not gibberish."

"It looks like it is."

"No. I think it's a language. You're sure of the letters?"

"I only transcribed them when I was sure, when I agreed with what was there. There's one more." He flipped a page. "D–e–o–s–space–M–I–N–space–e–o–r–d–b–y–r–g–e–n."

"The "D"s look like a backwards '6'."

"Yeah, kind of."

"I have a friend. She studies language. Etymology. I'd love for her to look at these. Just the words. If I showed her the pictures she'd just freak out."

Cy let that sit between them for a moment, then he pulled the notebook to him, ripped out a blank page, and produced a pen. "I'll copy them. There are only a few like this, so far."

Gloria clapped her hands together. "Anna will *love* this."

"Etymology," Cy muttered, copying. "Asterisms."

"If these are words, she'll figure it out."

Cy looked up at her, and Gloria raised her hand. "I know. Big secret. Want to spit on our palms and shake on it?"

Cy smiled. "How about I'll just trust you."

Sunday, November 3, 1974

Cy stopped at the kitchen door with a pillowcase of laundry. Kate, Brenda and Ben were seated around the table in varying degrees of wakefulness, eating breakfast. "I'm doing a load," he informed them. "Anybody have anything they want to throw in?"

Kate shook her head chewing.

"No thanks," Ben said, waving a piece of toast.

Brenda pointed her spoon at the pillowcase. "Are you doing underwear?"

"Yep."

"Then, nope."

Cy grinned. "Save me some milk, please," he said, and went down.

The vintage washer and dryer sat side by side along the south wall, next to the soapstone double deep sink. A variety of laundry products crowded the grimy shelf above. Cy dumped the pillowcase contents into the washer, then the pillowcase. He sprinkled in some detergent, set the dials, and slapped the big one to get it going.

He went around the furnace to his studio area. The *Dark*

Angel painting leaned against the wall, loosely covered by an old sheet. It was done. Done and dusted. He had a new painting on the easel now, a large landscape of cows wandering up a long hill in pre-dawn light. The previous evening, working on it, he had decided it sucked. This morning, at first look in dodgy shadow, he decided he didn't hate it quite so much. He pulled the cord on the overhead fluorescents, squinting in the sudden light, and stopped. One of his brushes lay on the rough concrete floor before the easel, fully loaded with fresh red paint. A ragged trail of color led from the small pile of it he had left on his palette the evening before to the edge, closest to where the brush lay on the floor.

What the hell?

He crouched and reached for the brush, but stopped again. Someone had used it to draw on the concrete, a shape, a shaky letter "c." A chill and shiver went through him. *A "C" for what? For Cyrus?* He looked at the brush, willing it to move, but it just lay there. The wet paint in its bristles glistened. "Talk to me," he whispered. He looked up, around, twisting. "Talk to me!"

He pounded up the stairs.

Kate stood at the sink, washing out her bowl. Ben and Brenda were still finishing their cereal. "Did anyone mess with my paints downstairs?"

Kate turned. "Of course not."

"Not me," Brenda said.

Ben shook his head. "What's up?"

"I found one of my brushes loaded with paint, laying on the floor."

Ben shrugged. "Maybe it rolled off your palette thingie."

"There's something painted on the floor, like somebody tried to write something."

Ben shook his head again. "Well it wasn't me."

"Me either." Kate racked her bowl, and reached for the dish towel.

"I won't even go down there at night." Brenda shuddered. "I hate centipedes."

"There aren't any centipedes down there."

Kate patted Brenda's shoulder as she passed her. "They give me the creeps too."

"Wait." Ben put down his spoon. "There's centipedes in the basement?"

Monday, November 4, 1974

The big studio room on the second floor of the FAB had emptied. All morning studio classes were over, so even the hallway outside was largely quiet. Professor Grakowski emerged from his little "between-studios" office, rubbing his hands, and stopped. "Mr. Barnaby," he said, "I'm astonished."

Cy stepped from behind his easel; he had two working brushes and a rag in his right hand, and the brush he was using in his left. He lowered them. "I wanted to keep working on this."

"Well that's...odd. Admirable, but still odd. I think even you would agree your current work-in-progress is not one of your better efforts."

Cy managed a small smile. "That's what I like about you, Professor."

"My insufferable, razor-edged honesty?"

"Yeah. And you're also always right: this thing sucks. But I want to finish it anyway."

"There's another class in here at one thirty."

"I know. I'll be gone by then."

Grakowski stood with his fists on his hips. Then he strode across the room, his well-worn boots clacking loudly on the polished concrete. He waved his hand as he approached. "Turn it around."

Cy moved the easel, screeching the locked wheels. They both stepped back and stood side by side. Grakowski crossed his arms, then brought his hand up to his chin, and scraped his forefinger across grey stubble. "I'm not going to discuss color. We've had that argument too many times already." He pointed.

"Your drawing of the pot is still off, along this side, here, do you see? Symmetry, Barnaby, symmetry. That line should go this way, *here*." He used a fingernail to scratch into the paint, then his hand came back to cradle his chin again, eyes darting. He pointed again. "The perspective is off with this book. You have two vanishing points, but only one is correct. The other is too low, too forced. It's a damn *book*, Barnaby, not a city block. This line should go here." Another scratch into the wet paint. "Do you see?"

If Cy had had a hand free he would have slapped his forehead. Of *course*. As it was, he just nodded. "Yeah," he said. "I do."

"The background is still fresh?"

"All of it is. There's new paint on the whole thing."

"Good. So fix it. And be out of here before the next class. And I can't help it: orange next to the blue, Mr. Barnaby. Orange next to the *blue*." Grakowski turned on his boot heel, and left Cy alone in the studio.

Cy looked at his painting. His shoulders sagged. He looked across the room to the clock, then back to the painting. "Orange next to the blue," he muttered, and turned the easel back around.

At a quarter after one he began scraping his palette clean, and washing his brushes in his battered can of murky turps.

"My my! Cyrus Barnaby, right? What are *you* doing here?"

He looked up. Betsy Moone. The one who had nearly stripped in the concourse, the one who had smiled at him. His apparently not-so-secret crush. *Waaay out of my league.* "Just leaving," he said.

She looked at his painting with a curious smile. "You've done better." Then she went past him, trailing a musky scent of patchouli, to the easels by the north windows, and dropped her black leather satchel before one. He capped his turps, and began shoving his brushes and paints into his rucksack. She glanced over her shoulder. "What, no comeback?"

Instead of replying he took his painting off the easel with

one hand, grabbed his palette with the other, and racked them.

She followed him to the racks, and pulled out her canvas. Cy saw a flash of underpainting: sienna and umber washes and broad, sketchy lines, a naked model against rough, draped cloth. She saw him looking and turned the painting so he could see. "Curious?"

That she could actually paint? Yes, actually. "It's pretty good."

"Wow, a compliment. I'll take it."

She stepped close to him, her bracelets jangling, that patchouli insolent in his nose. "I saw you on the concourse the other day, watching my performance piece. Watching me." She whispered in his ear, "I was watching you too, you know."

He pulled away. "That was the point, right?"

A smile curled her dark crimson lips. She stepped close enough to bite his ear if she wanted, "I think you're too shy for the bad girls."

He pulled away again, turning from the dancing laughter in her emerald green eyes. "I don't know what you're talking about."

She came to him again, put a hand into his hair, and ran her fingers down the back of his neck. "I know, because I'm a bad girl." She moved closer, her hip touching his.

"Whoa, sorry! Interrupting something?" An anonymous student, canvas in hand, stood at the nearest hallway door.

Betsy pirouetted away, laughing. "Just pillow talk, Vinny."

Cy's cheeks were hot, his heart pounding blood in his ears. He grabbed his rucksack, crossed the concrete floor without feeling it. "Out of the way," he muttered to the student at the door, and shouldered by him, into the high, wide hallway.

Tuesday, November 5, 1974

The doorbell rang.

"Door!" Brenda yelled, from her room.

"So go get it!" Kate yelled, from hers.

Cy capped his yellow highlighter, got up from his desk, and said, "Thank you for getting the door, Cyrus, you're such a dear," as he crossed the landing to the stairs.

"Smooches!" Kate sang after him.

"Barfing!" Brenda rejoined.

The doorbell rang again as he grasped the doorknob. "Hold your horses," he began, swinging the door wide, then, "Oh. Hi."

Gloria stood before him, bundled in a fur-trimmed ski jacket and a seriously long rainbow scarf. She pointed to the hippie "Our House" sign beside the door. "It says 'Please ring,'" she said. "I'm freezing my buns off. Can I come in?"

"Sure, of course." Cy stepped aside, pointing to the living room, and followed her.

Gloria unwound the scarf, and tossed it and her coat on the end of the front couch. "I've got it," she said.

"The translation?"

She nodded vigorously as they both sat.

From upstairs, Kate: "Offer her some tea, dumbass!"

Cy screwed up his face. "Sorry; I live in a crazy-house with crazy people. Would you...?"

"No thanks, I'm not a tea person." Gloria raised her voice, "Thanks anyway!"

"You're welcome! Closing my door now."

Gloria grinned at Cy. "Who's that?"

"That's Kate."

"Good friend of yours?"

"Sometimes I wonder. So...the translation?"

She fished in a pocket and extracted a folded piece of paper. It was the page he had ripped out of his notebook. "You are not going to believe this." She unfolded it and gave it to him.

Each of the lines of gibberish he had given her the previous week had words written under them. He looked up. "Your entomologist friend?"

"Etymologist. Entomology is bugs. Yeah. Anna. She nailed it. Took one look and knew right away."

"So it's a language?"

"Are you ready? Old English."

"*What?*"

"Can you believe it? An extinct Celtic or Anglo-Saxon language, or anyway whatever English used to be, a thousand years ago."

"But that's…crazy."

"Crazier than messages *in* dead people, *from* dead people?"

"Point taken." He read the gibberish in his head, *baecern beO IC.* Then, aloud, "'Where am I?'"

"Definitely a question, Anna said."

The second: *SE angnesse forjigeseeft.* "'The–my–pain persists.'"

"'Persists' was as close as she could get. Almost, 'My pain is forever.'"

"The third one is the creepiest." *deos MIN eordbyrgen.* "Is this my grave?"

"'Grave' or 'corpse pit.' Lovely, isn't it?"

Cy stared at the paper for a long moment. "Eight hundred years ago." He shook his head slowly. "Doesn't make sense."

Gloria gave him a crooked smile, "No more than messages written in blood capillaries, Cyrus."

Cy folded the paper. "Did you tell this friend of yours where the Old English came from?"

"Absolutely not. This is between you, me, Prof Baylor, and the loony bin. Anyway." She bounced to her feet, "Gotta go." She grabbed up her jacket and scarf.

"I owe you," Cy said, rising. "Again."

She grinned over her scarf. "You bet you do. And we're not just talking coffee this time."

Wednesday, November 6, 1974

"Come!"

Cy closed Professor Baylor's office door behind him. "Sorry I'm late." He unslung his rucksack. "Professor Porterfield wouldn't let us go until she made a *point*."

"Today of all days!" Baylor rapped his fingers on his desk. "Today of all days!" He stood with a grunt, and several papers slid from his desk to the floor. He stepped on them. "Come. Here. Follow me. I have it ready."

"It" was a shallow metal pan, sitting alone on the oak library table under the windows. A large white cloth napkin was draped over it.

"Do you need a chair?"

How many times had he asked that? Every time, that's how many. And Cy's reply, every time, was the same. "No, Professor, I like to work standing up."

"Of course, of course." The professor was like a little boy, now, eager to show off his newest toy. He grasped the napkin on two corners and lifted it away.

Cy wrinkled his nose at the little whiff of formaldehyde. It was a fresh human meninges caul, of course, pinned to a dissecting mat. The tracery pattern of brown capillaries in the tissue was especially vivid. "Nice," he said.

"Fresh," Baylor said. "Fresh this morning. I allowed Miss Halliday to do the staining."

"It's fine," Cy said. He opened his rucksack, and as he took out his paintbox, watercolor paper block, and brushes, Baylor fetched him a beaker of water and roll of paper towels. "There," he said. "Now I will leave you alone."

The folded piece of paper of translated messages was in Cy's pocket, but he hesitated showing it to Baylor. The subject of the messages hidden in the caul capillary patterns was still "not a subject for discussion." "Thanks," he said instead.

Baylor returned to his desk.

A half-hour later, Cy looked up from his painting, and found the professor watching him from across the office. "Sir?"

"It is nothing. I am just…envious, young man."

"Of painting?" Cy waved his free hand over the watercolor. "It just takes practice, like anything else."

"Practice." Baylor nodded, with a wistful, almost sad

expression. "And youth." He turned his chair fully around. "I will tell you something. I will share. When I was young, painting and medicine were my twin passions, both important, equally important."

"Why did you pick medicine?"

Baylor barked a single laugh. "Because it was the easier of the two."

Cy hesitated. *What the hell.* "I looked at those portfolios in the library downstairs. Are those yours? The last one, the newest one. Did you do those paintings? When you were younger?"

Baylor allowed a long moment of silence to stretch. Then he nodded brusquely. "When I was a young man, yes, some of them." He held out his right hand, palm down. "Can you see this? The shaking? You are too polite, but it is there." He lowered his hand. "So I gave up one of my passions, the more difficult one. And, eventually, for the same reason, the other as well."

"But you were a surgeon. A neurosurgeon. A famous one."

Laughter-lines creased around Baylor's eyes. "Our young Mr. Roth telling tales again, eh?"

Cy decided to keep going. "So you did the caul paintings because you saw things in the tissue?"

Silence. The professor was looking at him, but he *wasn't*, at the same time. Cy waited.

"All animals are pattern seekers, Mr. Barnaby," Baylor said finally. "Humans are no exception. We take comfort in our patterns: in the layout of our homes, our streets, in the fabrics we wear. And in words as well. Balanced sentences, poems. Even in faces. Some might say particularly in faces. Symmetry, to some extent, denotes beauty, eh? We seek them out, these symmetries, these patterns." He looked away, and window light reflected off his glasses. "Sometimes what we find is real. Sometimes what we find is not."

Asterisms. "But I've seen them," Cy said. "They're real."

"Perhaps." Baylor looked back to him, and nodded to the brush in his hand. "You are drying out, Mr. Barnaby. Please continue, while you still have the light."

Instead, Cy pulled the folded paper out of his pocket, and walked it over to the professor. Baylor peered at it over his glasses, then took it from him. He opened it, and moved his glasses up his nose. When he finished reading he refolded it, and handed it back. "So you have seen them all, eh?"

"You gave me that note."

"Ah. Of course." Baylor nodded slowly.

"I had to have some of them translated."

"You needn't have bothered the etymologists. I had that done years ago." The professor tented his fingers and peered over them, a sudden focus in his eyes. "And did your comrades in arms translate the Akkadian mutterings as well?"

"The what?"

"One can find perfectly legible cuneiform babbling on any chicken coop floor, Mr. Barnaby."

Cy gestured back to the table, to his art materials scattered across it. "I don't know why you don't just photograph them."

Baylor was quiet for a moment, then he nodded. "Here," he said. "Come." He heaved himself upright, dusted cigarette ash from his tie, and motioned Cy to follow him. They went to the file cabinets. Baylor chose a drawer, and extracted a thick folder. "Now," he said, and motioned with it. They went to the far corner of the office, where a small soapstone lab table and an old, round-shouldered refrigerator sat side by side. As Baylor found room for the folder on the lab table, he pointed to the refrigerator. "Open, please?"

"There's a lock on the handle."

Eh? Oh, of course." Baylor produced a set of keys, and opened it himself. The smell of cold stale meat and formaldehyde assailed Cy. The refrigerator contained a large metal rack of shelves, each shelf containing small dissection pans, two dozen pans at least, all of them covered by plastic lids.

"Cauls?"

Baylor had shuffled back to the open folder. "Yes. Of course. Here. Look."

The folder contained a disordered pile of large color

photographs. Baylor chose one at random, flipped it over, and read the label there. "Be so kind, Mr. Barnaby, remove the tray numbered seventeen."

Cy found one numbered sixteen, and pulled out the one behind it. "Seventeen," he said.

Baylor took the tray from him, and placed it carefully on the lab table beside the selected photograph. He removed the plastic cover, and waved Cy to join him. "Now, what do you see?"

"It's a meninges caul, and a photograph of it."

"Indeed."

"So you do have them photographed!"

Baylor nodded. "Without fail."

"Then why do you need me to paint them?"

Baylor raised a finger. "Because. A moment." He went around Cy to the flat files below the windows. "The number again, please?"

"Seventeen."

Baylor returned with a typewriter-size piece of thick paper. A painting, a watercolor of a caul. He placed it beside the photograph. Cy bent over it. "Did you do this?"

Baylor chuckled. He waved his hand over the painting, the photograph, and the caul in the tray. "Compare, please. Take your time. Study."

"Well, the painting is more like the caul than the photo. This is all kind of old, though, right?"

"Old enough, yes."

"The photo looks like it lost some red. The blues are more prominent."

"Photographic dyes are not permanent," Baylor said, nodding. "But Mr. Winsor and Mr. Newton, eh? Keep their paints out of the sunlight, keep them safe, and the paint, it does not lie. Why do you paint my cauls? *This* is why." He recovered the tray and returned it to the refrigerator. "So, now. You have a new specimen. Finish painting it, please. Do Mr. Winsor and Mr. Newton proud."

They returned to the front of the office, Baylor to his desk,

Cy to the library table.

Ten minutes later, forgetting for just a moment that he wasn't alone, Cy gasped, "What the *hell!*"

Behind him, a chair squeaked, and Professor Baylor's voice rose querulously. "What is the matter?" He hurried over. "What?"

"I can read it," Cy said. "I can read this one. Look." Cy's voice shook. He took in a breath. "Look," he said again, and pointed with his pencil. "It says: 'WHERE AM I' there, and there: 'IM COLD.'"

Baylor looked from the caul to Cy's drawing, then again. "This is a 'D'? You're sure?"

"I'm just painting what's there."

Baylor looked from one to the other again, and then again. "And what about this, this word here?" He pointed.

"I'm...I'm not sure." *Why am I stammering?* The word there, written in blood vessels, was why. "It starts with an 'S.'"

"And ends with one as well. SIRIUS. A Latin word, I believe. Like the star, eh? Curious."

Cy stared down at the caul, laboring to breathe. He was nearly overcome by an urge to drop his pencil, abandon his brushes and paints, and just run away. Instead, he stood motionless, silent, the word clear in his mind's eye. The word he was sure was meant for him, and only him. The capillaries spelled SIRIUS.

Serious Cyrus.

His mother's voice, echoing down the years: "Will you just look at him, Dan? He's just so adorable! Our serious little Cyrus. Our little star!"

Cy looked at the words, all of them, for him.

Where am I? I'm cold. Sirius. I'm cold.

I'm cold, Cyrus.

The sun had set, and the stars were out in full force when Cy emerged from the medical college. He struck out across the quad, following a well-worn path in the grass. Sirius. First Old English, now Latin. Two dead languages. Crazy. Just, crazy. *I'm cold, Cyrus.*

Like the slap on his cheek, the poke in his ribs, and the shadow in the corner that was there, and then gone. Like the attempt at painting a "C" on the basement floor. And the weeping, from somewhere not *here*. Especially that.

It can't be you, Mom. Can it?

He stopped in the center of the quad, and a sudden ache in his chest almost made him gasp for breath. It was an ache in his heart that *hurt*. It was a sadness that was nearly overwhelming, almost suffocating.

Why are you haunting me?

He turned to look up into the southeast sky. Orion was rising, well above the line of trees and houses edging the campus. And at Orion's heels ran Canis Major, the hunting dog with the brightest star in the sky for its eye: Sirius. The Dog Star. Cy clenched his teeth, and blinked back sudden tears. *Where am I? I'm cold. Sirius. I'm cold.*

"Me too, Mom," he whispered, as an uncontrollable shiver wracked him. *Me too.*

Friday, November 9, 1974

"And this," Cy said, holding the door open, "is my room."

Gloria stepped past him. "Cozy."

"It's only forty bucks a month."

"What a deal." She took off her ski jacket.

"Here." Cy hung it off the back of his desk chair, followed by his own.

Gloria looked around, then sat cross-legged on the floor by the bed. Cy grabbed his sketchbook from the desk, and followed her example.

She rubbed her hands together. "So? Show me."

"It's just the pencil sketch. Baylor always keeps the watercolors." He flipped through the sketchbook to the last one, the newest one, and passed it to her.

Gloria studied the drawing for almost a full minute. Then,

with her long forefinger, she began tracing. "S–I, or maybe Y–R–I, definitely, U–S." She looked up to him. "Sirius. That's a star name."

"Yeah. I know."

She looked back down. "The rest is clear. I–M–C–O–L–D. I've seen that before. They're always cold." She looked up again. "This is from a new one, you said?"

"The newest. I just did it Wednesday."

Someone came bounding up the stairs. Ben, carrying a girl on his back. She had long, pale-blonde hair, and a lit joint dangling from her lips. She took it out and exhaled. "Hello!"

Gloria pointed at Ben. "I know you. Pre-med, right?"

Ben grinned and panted. "I'd bow, but…"

"But he'd drop me on my ass!" The blonde girl laughed.

Somehow Ben got them both into his room and closed the door.

"Weed," Gloria said, "can be a wonderful thing."

More laughter from Ben's room, then music, Zeppelin, turned up high.

Gloria raised the sketchbook. "Back to this, please. So why the name of a star? Is it important?"

"It was a nickname my mom gave me. She used to call me Serious Cyrus."

Gloria's eyes narrowed with sudden concern. "Wait a minute. Your mom…."

"She died when I was five. My dad too. Car accident."

"Oh dear." Gloria closed the sketchbook, put her arms around him, and hugged him. "I'm sorry," she said, against his ear. When she released him she still held on, gripping his shoulders. "And you think she is trying to talk to you? Through the cauls?"

"I don't know what to think, except that…except that, yeah, she's haunting me."

"Oh Cyrus." She hugged him again, and he hugged her back. "It's…nuts," he said, into her hair. "It's crazy. It's driving *me* crazy."

Her softness, her warmth, brought his cheek to hers, then his lips to her lips. They kissed slowly, tentatively, almost chastely. Then they separated. Gloria ran a finger down his cheek. "You're sweet," she whispered. "But, really, I'm old enough to be your—"

"Aunt?"

"Ew! I was going to say older sister." But she smiled, and he smiled back.

The front door opened, closed, and someone new came up the stairs. Cy and Gloria put more space between them. This time it was Kate, carrying a pile of books on her hip.

She turned at her door, keys in her free hand. "Oh," she said, "Hello."

Gloria got to her feet. "You must be Kate."

Kate crossed the landing to Cy's doorway. "And you must be…"

"Gloria. The one who doesn't do tea. And I really must be going." She picked her ski jacket off the desk chair, and turned back to Cy. "We'll talk about this." She touched his shoulder. "We're good?"

"Yeah." Cy got up. "Yeah, we're good."

"Good." She shrugged into her jacket. "Nice meeting you in person, Kate."

"Same here. Come again."

Gloria smiled, and made for the stairs.

"So," Kate said, hefting her textbooks a little higher on her hip as the front door closed.

Cy spread his hands. "So?"

She turned and re-crossed the landing, jingling her keys. "Just…so."

Friday, November 15, 1974

Cy and Kate *("This is not a date, Cyrus.*
Who said anything about a date?

I've just never been to one of these. Plus, I'm in the painting, right?
Right.
So…No date.
No date.
Good.

Good.") spent the half-hour before the doors officially opened on the Winter Student Juried Exhibit–a half-hour of students, faculty, alumni, townies, and everyone else involved in the Local Art Scene all standing with little paper plates and plastic cups, sipping cheap wine and nibbling anonymous canapés, cheese cubes and crackers, while discussing absolutely pure absolute bullshit in quiet, pointed voices–with everyone else in the wide hallway connecting the Elting Art Gallery to the Fine Arts Building. A cold wind ruffled hairdos, dresses and table coverings every time one of the outside doors opened, and caused more than one person to bounce on their heels, and check their watches. Cy discovered a paper napkin stuck to the bottom of his tennis shoe, and he scraped it off on the rim of a pot between overhanging hosta leaves. "Classy," Kate said, handing him a cup of wine.

He downed half of it. "Wow that's bad."

She took a sip of hers, and grimaced. "So this TA told you there was going to be a surprise?"

"Yeah." Cy tossed the napkin and cup into a trash receptacle. "Professor Grakowski was acting weird with me this week too."

"Grakowski is one of your painting professors?"

"Yeah." He scanned the crowd, nodded to a passing student, and then another. Only the second one nodded back. "He said he'd be here."

"So…" Kate began again.

"So the TA helped hang the show." Cy shrugged. "Maybe he hung my painting upside-down."

"But that doesn't make sense. He wasn't serious, was he?"

"I'm joking." Cy gave her his pity-me face.

A ripple went through the crowd. "Doors opening,"

someone said, "thank God."

As they all moved forward, Kate noticed the paint smears on the ass of Cy's jeans. "Nice of you to dress up for the occasion."

Cy twisted, tried to look over his shoulder. "What?"

"Hey, I put on a *skirt* for this."

"And you look—"

"Wonderful, my dear," interrupted an elderly gentleman in a suit, winking at Kate as he passed them.

"Yeah," Cy pointed. "What he said. You look great."

They both shivered in the curtain of heat as they passed through the double doors. "Wow," Kate said, "big room."

The main display area of the gallery was a large, unobstructed space with a high traycase ceiling. The walls were taken up for the most part with the truly large paintings and assemblages, dozens of pieces, all of them, from what Cy could see, derivative crap. A maze of tall, freestanding display panels, connected at right angles in twos and threes, filled the central area of the gallery. Paintings of more manageable size—the bulk of the show—had been hung on them. Large floor sculptures, and smaller ones on pedestals, filled the corners and open spaces between the standing panels. A row of glass cases along the rear wall displayed gold, silver and copper jewelry, and ceramic pieces.

The first freestanding panel faced the gallery doors, and the single painting mounted on it was the first one anyone entering would see. The painting was nearly three feet across and six feet high, a representational oil of a—

Ô noir ange...

"Oh my God Cy," Kate hissed. "There I am! I mean, there it is!"

A small cluster of people had already formed around Cy's painting. Someone was attempting to read the French title aloud. Kate elbowed her way in, but Cy stayed back. The elderly man in the suit was there, and he bent his head to say something to Kate. She replied, first pointing to herself, and then, turning, to

Cy standing apart. The man nodded to him, smiling. Cy felt a cold breeze wash through him, not from outside, but from within. *This is not going to go well.* Still… *shit.* He took a deep breath, and strode forward.

"Here he is," Kate said to the man, grabbing Cy's arm. "This is Cy. Cyrus Barnaby."

The gentleman offered his hand, and Cy shook it. "You've certainly done your homework, young man."

What to say? Something simple. "Thanks."

"The Rooker," the gentleman continued. "Well deserved. Well deserved indeed. Congratulations."

Cy felt the floor fall out beneath him, and he held Kate's arm for support. "The *what?*"

Someone beside Cy giggled. Another pointed, and then Cy saw it: two printed cards next to the painting: the title card, which all the pieces had, and another above it, rimmed in metallic blue, with "August F. Rooker Prize" hand-written on it in black ink, in calligraphic script.

Kate looked at the card with wide eyes. "What's the Rooker Prize?"

"It's…" Cy began, then shook his head. "I don't believe it."

The gentleman gripped his shoulder. "There are a variety of prizes at shows like these, young lady. Best In Media, Jury Selection, Best In Show of course…and then there is the Rooker Prize. The last time they awarded a Rooker was, let me see, five years ago, I believe."

"I'm still not getting it. What does Cy win?"

"Money, probably," someone said.

Kate's eyes grew even wider. "Cy…?"

Cy waved his hand dismissively. "It's nothing."

"It's hardly nothing, Mr. Barnaby." The gentleman turned to Kate. "You should be very proud of your boyfriend."

"Well I am. But he's not, I mean, we're just friends—hey!"

Cy was already through the doors of the gallery, dodging people in the courtyard. Gone.

He spent the next two hours wandering in the evening gloom. He walked Main Street from east to west, from the Jack-in-the-Box by the Middle School, past every single bar, store, restaurant and head shop all the way to the river. Continuing over the trestle bridge to the snow-covered cornfields beyond was not an option, however. A left turn led to the neighborhood of the town's pricier homes, and eventually back to the campus. A right turn followed the river-walk, past the abandoned railroad station, then the ancient Huguenot stone house ruins. It was also in the general direction of Our House, of home.

He went right.

The cinders from the tracks had migrated over time down to the river-walk path. Mingled with crusty snow, the hard crunch under his tennis shoes made a satisfying sound. The evening sky appeared brighter on the gently moving water. Crows called, from one bank to the other, over the quieter sounds of smaller birds, talking over one another in the tangle of roots and brambles along the bank, all of them settling in for the night. He hesitated kicking a particularly large cinder, then picked it up. For just a moment he considered throwing it at the railroad station, above him in the shadows, maybe scare the bejesus out of whatever hobos or ghosts lived there, but he threw it instead out over the river, hearing a satisfying "plunk" above the quiet rush of the water.

He kept to the path until it branched, and followed the new path away from the riverbank, up the slope. When he came upon the three granite steps next to the old octagonal chapel, he knew his destination was here: the town's original cemetery. He paused at the top step to make sure no one was already in there, making out among the weathered, tilting stones. *Too cold*, he decided. He made his way to his favorite spot, the overturned slab of grey Catskill slate with Phillip Lefevre's name chiseled in it, just a faintly uneven surface under his fingers as he brushed off the snow, and sat. The cemetery was small, intimate, maybe fifty graves in all. He had painted it several times. "The people from the city love this stuff," a local gallery manager had gushed when he showed her the first ones. "I'll take everything you do of that old boneyard."

Cy frowned in the darkness, looking west to the harvested cornfields beyond the river, and the black ribbon of mountains against the clear, indigo sky. *The Rooker Prize.* He still couldn't believe it. The Rooker Prize meant his tuition would be paid for, probably through his MFA years, if he stayed. It meant collectors would start raising their noses, sniffing in his direction. It meant he didn't need his aunt and uncle's support. It meant he could finally do it all on his own.

So why am I unhappy?

"I did it, Mom, Dad," he said in a quiet voice. "You don't have to worry about me any more. I'll be fine." The evening swallowed his words, making him wonder if he had actually spoken them aloud.

Why am I still so sad? Why does it feel like my core, my guts, are all rotted out?

An acorn fell beside him, rattling across the stone. He looked up. *Go to sleep, squirrel.*

He stood. Time to go home, and do the same. He made his way out between the darkness and the stones, to an empty street splashed with streetlights.

In minutes he reached the path alongside the old stable garage to the parking area behind Our House. The kitchen and dining room lights threw long, golden swaths across the back lot, revealing Kate's and Brenda's cars. He stopped abruptly at the corner of the garage; there was a light on in his bedroom. *What the hell?*

He wove through the cars, took the back stoop in two steps, and almost banged his knee getting the kitchen door open.

"And here he is! Mr. Rooker Prize winner!"

Ben, Kate, and Brenda sat around the kitchen table. Ben and Brenda had bottles of beer in hand, and Kate cradled her mug of tea. All three raised their drinks in salute, chorusing, "Congratulations!" Then Kate said, "And thanks for leaving me in the lurch, buddy-boy."

"The light in my room is on," Cy said.

"Um." Kate lowered her mug. "You have a visitor."

Cy went by them, down the front hallway to the stairs.

"And you're welcome!" Ben yelled after him. "Jeez!" He turned to Kate. "And you actually wore a *skirt*?"

He found his door open just a crack, and heard his stereo's radio tuned to the FM rock station in Woodstock, playing low.

Betsy Moone sat cross-legged on his bed. Her boots were on the floor, along with most of the rest of her clothing. And he saw, again, her impossibly green eyes.

"Close the door," she said, softly.

He did.

"Lock it?"

He did that, too.

She reached over, bracelets sliding, chiming, and turned the music up. "I'm loud sometimes."

Saturday, November 16, 1974

Cy entered the kitchen, squinting at the wall clock. Kate sat at the table with a bowl of cereal and a smug smile. He nodded to her, got bread and a plate from his cabinet, and a knife from the communal drawer, and frowned into the open refrigerator. "Can I borrow some butter?"

"You can *have* some of my butter."

"Please, it's too early." He put his bread in the toaster, then dropped into the chair opposite her.

Kate put her spoon in the bowl. "So."

"So?"

"So congrats again on winning the Rooker Prize, you ungrateful son of a bitch."

Cy nodded. "Point taken. I apologize."

She looked down at her bowl, then up. "So…the brunette."

"What brunette?"

"The brunette in black silk and leather and waay too much makeup who paid you a visit last night."

"Ah, that brunette. That's Betsy. Betsy Moone."

"She didn't look like a Betsy. She looked more like a Morticia."

"Well, that's her name."

"I think I'll call her Morticia the Coffin Lady."

"The what?" Cy couldn't help but smile. "*Coffin* Lady?"

"So are you guys..." Kate waved her finger around, "you know..."

Cy's toast popped up. He rose to get it, plate in hand. "We're fellow art students."

"Aha. Fellow art students."

"Friends." Cy was generous with Kate's butter. "We're just friends."

"Just friends."

He sat back down. "Can you please stop repeating everything I say?"

"I just never had you down as a 'slam-bam-thank-you-ma'am' kind of guy."

"I'm not, but...things happen. Sometimes new people happen. New friends happen."

"Friends like...The Coffin Lady?"

Cy pointed at her with his butter knife. "I wouldn't say that to her face. I don't know what she might do."

"Oh I pretty much know exactly what she'd do, Cyrus." Kate smiled sweetly.

"I mean really, they did it all night long," Brenda said, passing through the kitchen, bundled up for a walk to campus. "I'm just on the other side of the goddamn wall for chrissakes, Cyrus." She opened the back door, then turned. "I just hope she pukes in her hair this weekend."

"Amen, sister," Kate said.

Brenda gave Cy a meaningful look, "And you still have dirty dishes from yesterday in the sink," then the back door banged shut behind her.

Cy took a bite of toast. "Coffin Lady," he said. "I have to admit, that's pretty good."

Kate pointed to the sink.

"I'll do them," Cy said. "I promise."

Monday, November 18, 1974

Four of the five long tables in the medical college library were occupied, so Cy claimed the end chair of the fifth, hung his coat and rucksack on it, and placed his sketchbook before him, unopened.

Gloria, seated behind the reference desk at the other end of the room, had an open book before her, and apparently hadn't seen him enter.

He made to get up three different times, but every time he tried, someone approached the reference desk first to ask a question. All three times Gloria's answers were long, and two required her to enter the stacks to retrieve books. Finally, Cy saw an opportunity, and took it.

"I tried to call you earlier," he whispered.

She closed her book on a finger. "I was busy."

"Is something wrong?"

"Nothing's wrong. Everything's fine."

"Did I do something?"

She sighed.

"What did I do?"

"This isn't the place, Cy."

Cy leaned on her desk, lowering his voice to a whisper. "So where's the place, then? You didn't meet me for coffee like we planned, then you didn't answer the phone—"

Gloria's voice was barely a hiss: "I was busy."

"So...you're avoiding me? Is that it?"

She sighed again.

"If I just knew what it was you think I did..."

"You didn't do anything, okay?" She lowered her voice even further. "It's that crazy bitch you're screwing."

Betsy. "Betsy Moone?"

"That her name? I'll stick with crazy bitch, thank you."

"How do you even know her?"

"I don't. I never saw her before."

"But I never mentioned you. I never–" Cy's voice cracked in exasperation. "Really…"

"All I know is she told me to lay off. She said *she* had you, and she wasn't sharing."

"But that's crazy. Listen, she doesn't speak for me."

"Keep your voice *down*." Gloria looked past him. "Just so you know, your Betsy Moone is the craziest nut job I think I've ever met. You should–" She stopped, put both her hands up, palms out, and shook her head.

"I should what?"

"It's none of my business."

"I should *what?*"

"Look, I'm up for a TA slot this summer. It's important. I'm not about to have it messed up by the Betsy Moones of this world. You can screw all the crazy girlfriends you want, just leave me out of it."

"She's not my girlfriend."

Gloria raised her hands again. "Whatever. I have too much to lose right now. I'm sorry, Cy." She looked past him again, and smiled. "Yes, can I help you?"

"I don't want to–" began a voice over Cy's shoulder.

"Oh no," Gloria said, with a dismissive wave, "We're done. How can I help you?"

Cy had nothing left to do but wheel away, trying not to trip over anything or bump into anyone, as he returned to his seat, gathered up his things, and left.

His bedroom door was unlocked and partly open. Cy rattled his door knob. *What the hell?* Behind him, Kate called from her room, "She was here, but she left. The Coffin Lady. You really should lock your door, you know."

"I did this time. I think I did." Betsy's patchouli scent still hung in the air of his room. Part of him got involuntarily excited, but the rest of him was simply and thoroughly pissed-off. He turned his doorknob back and forth again. *Why had she come, and then left?*

He went in, and stopped a step from his desk. He counted only four sketchbooks. The fifth one, the newest one, the one containing the cadaver sketches and caul drawings, was missing. "Son of a bitch," he whispered. He opened each of the four sketchbooks just to be sure. "Son of a bitch!" He was out of his room and across the landing to the stairs in three strides.

"Hey," Kate called after him as he pounded downstairs. "You didn't lock your door!"

He yelled back over his shoulder, "What's the point?"

Bliss Hall. Bliss the all-girl dorm. Bliss, the Nunnery. A resident assistant was supposed to man the lobby desk at all times, but the desk was empty except for a scattering of flyers and a bent Pepsi can. A few girls on lobby sofas gave Cy the eye as he passed through to the center stairwell, but he ignored them.

Betsy had said something about being able to see Cemetery Pond from the second floor, so he went into the east hallway, closest to the pond. The hallway was awash in smells of perfume, cigarettes and incense. The music coming from open doors mixed Joni Mitchell with Neil Young, the Doobies with Zeppelin. He stopped at the first open door, and knocked to get the attention of the two girls inside. "I'm looking for Betsy Moone's room?"

The girls exchanged looks. "Down at the end," one of them said. "You can't miss it," added the other. They both giggled.

The last door on the right was closed and bare of any decoration, not even a message pad. It was also painted black. He hesitated.

"Go on, hon," a girl half a step out of her door across the hall said, watching him, "don't be shy," to more giggling from behind her.

He knocked. From inside, in a sing-song voice: "It's open, Cyrus."

Everything in Betsy's dorm room was black, the walls, curtains, desk, even the ceiling. Betsy sat on her bed, wearing only a black silk blouse and panties. His sketchbook was open before her. "This is freaking incredible," she said, pointing. "I had no idea it would be this insane."

He strode across the room and grabbed the sketchbook, slapping it shut against his chest. "It's private. It's none of your goddamn business."

"Cyrus. Seriously. You know what you have there?"

"I'm working for a professor. He's paying me. Like I said: private."

"Professor who?"

"None of your goddamn business."

"He's in the medical college? Baylor, I bet. I've heard about him."

She truly had nothing on but the blouse and panties. Her toenails were as blood-red as her fingernails; her hair and bed sheets were all one, all silken, all black. She said, "Those drawings, the oddly shaped ones, are those the brain cauls?"

He scowled at her, his mouth closed in a tight line.

"They're from cadavers. I *know*, Cyrus." She leaned forward, revealing the soft white curves of her breasts. "You're communicating with the dead. That's what it is, isn't it?" Her emerald eyes were hungry on him, eating him from the inside out.

"Professor Baylor's not sure."

"So it is Baylor!" She laughed. "Oh Cyrus! Close the door."

"I'm not—"

"Cyrus." She rose, her long hair falling in tousled waves down her shoulders, around her face, framing it. Softly: "*Close the door.*"

He did so, and when he turned her breath washed his cheek, and her lips found his. Her kiss was urgent, pushing him back against the door, the sketchbook dropping as he held her, his hands lost in her hair, in the smooth arch of her back. The lock turned with a snap, then her arms were around him as well, pulling him tight to her, her thigh slipping between his, tongue searching, deep, her mouth consuming his.

She broke the kiss finally, temporarily. "Do you have any idea," she breathed, her lips again brushing his, "how hot this makes me?"

They lay in the dark in the damp, black sheets. She caressed his flaccid penis in a lazy motion, and murmured, "They sound sad."

He made a questioning sound.

"The messages. The dead, talking."

He gently squeezed her left breast in his hand, his fingers feeling the nipple tighten.

She ignored his caress. "Like they're lost, somewhere. Somewhere where the dead go, where they *really* go. God I wish I knew where it was."

"Purgatory. Heaven. Hell."

She snorted. "Warmed over Bronze Age myths. Organized religion doesn't have a *clue*."

Outside, in the hallway, someone ran past chanting "Yeah, yeah, yeah!" Old Beatles music swelled, then cut off as a door opened and closed with a slam.

Betsy rolled onto her side to turn on her bedside lamp. "This is important, Cyrus. Really important."

The slap, the poke, the weeping, the shadow in the corner, *Sirius*… "I know."

"There has to be a way to talk back. I mean, all we have is a one-way conversation. They're doing all the talking. 'I'm cold,' 'it's dark.'" She reached down beside the bed and brought up a bottle of red wine, half-empty. "Can you reach the cups?"

Cy saw a short stack of paper cups on the desk. "But there's no way to do that," he said, reaching. "All you can do is talk into the air, and hope someone hears." He held two cups out. "And even then, how do you connect the question you ask with the tissue the answer comes in? You can't dissect everyone."

"But don't you wish you could?" She poured. "Wouldn't you like to talk to them, to someone?"

Of course, dammit. An image flashed in his head of a newspaper clipping, a photo found in one of the boxes stored on the third floor of his aunt and uncle's brownstone: *the crumpled wreck of his parents' car on the side of the highway, a riot of footprints in the snow, a pale-faced policeman catching the photographer's flash in both eyes as he raised his hand.* He took a sip of the sour wine. "I don't know," he said.

"Well I do." Betsy downed her wine in one long swallow. "My mother, my mom." She looked beyond the end of the bed, focused on nothing but the gathered shadows.

"I'm sorry you lost your mom."

She frowned. "It's like she's still out there, somewhere, still trying to, I don't know, be my mom. She's just…out of reach."

"When did she die?"

"Five years. I was fourteen." She looked at him briefly. "Car accident."

The cop was there again, still trying to raise his hand to protect the tangled, snow-covered wreck, with its grisly presents wrapped up tight, inside…

She gestured to his sketchbook on the floor by the door. "Then I saw them, your drawings, and it suddenly felt like maybe it was possible, like it was real, like maybe I could finally, actually talk to her."

"You miss her a lot."

"You have no idea." She was quiet for a moment, then she laughed. "Actually, you probably do."

"It was a long time ago."

She looked at him through her tousled hair, her green eyes catching the twilight. "You ever think about it? You know, dying?"

Yes. "No," he said.

"Dying so you can be with your parents?"

All the time. "No."

"Well I do. I think about it a lot. I'm obsessed." She flung her arms wide. "Black room, black clothes. Black heart."

"Just because you like black doesn't mean you want to die."

She shook her head. "I can't help thinking about it. About what's on the other side."

"You shouldn't think that way. You're talented. You're beautiful."

"So are you: talented, cute." She reached out, her fingernails trailing down his cheek, down his neck, her fingers spreading on his chest. "You think about it too; I know you do. Death, Cyrus, just has a bad rap."

He didn't reply.

She took his cup, and drained it. "I have to see them."

"Mine's the only sketchbook where—"

"No." She crumpled the cup and tossed it away. "I mean the real ones. The real cauls. You have to take me to the dissection rooms."

"What? No way. I'm not even allowed down there. There's no way I can get you in too." The thought of the cauls Professor Baylor kept in the refrigerator in his office bubbled up, but he fought the urge to tell her. "I would if I could," he lied. "Really."

"You're too sweet sometimes, you know?" She moved to kiss him, but he pulled away just enough for her lips to miss.

"You can't be tired. Not yet." Her hand found his penis, and it was already paying attention.

"It's not that." Cy put his hand on hers. "You have to stop bothering my friends."

"Who? The people at your rooming house? I barely said two words to them."

"Not them. Gloria."

"Who the hell is Gloria? I thought your friends were named Kate, or something."

"Gloria works in the library at the medical college."

Betsy stopped caressing him, betraying the careless tone in her voice. "How did I bother her?"

"You know how."

Her fingers tightened around him, and her eyes became bottomless. "She's too old for you, Cyrus. What is she, twenty-five or something?"

"She's a friend."

"I have friends too, but I'm not fucking all of them."

"That's it." He pushed her away, flung the sheet off, and swung his feet to the floor. *Why am I here? Why am I doing this?*

"Wait." Betsy reached to put her arms around him. "Wait. Please. I'm sorry." She nuzzled through his hair and kissed his neck. "Really. I'm sorry. I'm a bitch. I can't help it. I was wrong. Please forgive me." She kissed his neck again.

"Promise me," he said.

"Fine." Kiss. "I promise." Both of her hands burrowed into his crotch. "Ahh," she whispered.

He fell back to the bed. She tried to take his tee shirt off, "Why are you still wearing this?"

He pushed her hands away. "I have a scar."

"Ooh! Really? Show me."

"It's ugly."

"Scars are never ugly, baby. Is that why you always keep your shirt on when we have sex? Here." She pulled his tee shirt up before he could stop her. He moved instinctively to cover his abdomen, but she took his wrists and held them away. "I love it," she whispered. She pushed him onto his back, and proceeded to kiss and lick the jagged red knot traversing his belly.

He gasped. "That tickles."

"Just wait," she murmured, climbing onto him.

Later, with a waxing crescent moon peeking through the window curtains, he said, "I really have to go. I have a psych quiz to study for."

She rubbed her nose against his neck. "Can't you blow it off?"

"Not with my class average." He made to get up, but she held him back. "There was one thing I didn't get," she said.

"What do you mean?"

"In the sketchbook."

It still lay on the floor by the door.

She laid her head on his stomach, on his scar. "Sirius. The message that had the word Sirius in it. That's a star, right?"

He nodded even though she couldn't see it. "Brightest star in the sky."

"Why mention that? I mean, if these are really voices from death, why waste time talking about astronomy?"

He was silent for a long moment, then he said, quietly, "Because it's me."

"What?" She turned her head to look up at him. "You?"

"I'm Sirius. Serious Cyrus. It's a homonym. It's what my mom would call me when she was making fun. She would call me Serious Cyrus. She's the only one who did."

Betsy sat up, her hair tumbling across her face. "Your mom." Her voice was flat.

"Yeah." He looked at her, at the bedside light catching her eyes through her hair. "She and my dad were killed in a car accident when I was five, the accident that caused the scar. That's why I think it's her. *My* mom, talking to *me*. I think she's trying to tell me something."

"Tell you what?"

"I don't know." He shook his own hair out of his eyes. "I just know it's important."

Wednesday, April 13, 1960

The day before he finally left the hospital, he remembered being sat down on a thick, soft carpet in a room filled with toys: teddy bears, dolls, puzzles, a fire engine, a stuffed tiger, wood blocks scattered about, and being told to play with whatever he wanted. The woman retired to a chair in the corner, her clipboard on her lap.

He remembered just sitting there, not wanting to play with any of the toys, not wanting to do anything. Just sit.

Finally, the woman asked him, "What is it you want, Cyrus? Another toy?"

He remembered shaking his head, his cheeks long since empty of tears. "I want my mommy."

3

Wednesday, November 27, 1974

Uncle Fred and Aunt Carol's brownstone was two blocks west of Prospect Park, in a yet-to-be gentrified Brooklyn neighborhood of the same name. Home, since Cy was five. Now it had become the place he came back to on holidays and summer break. Every time he returned, he saw the sandstone block on the side of the front stoop with "1886" carved into it, and every time he did the math: this time, this Thanksgiving, the number was eighty-eight. Eighty-eight years old; full of memories and history. Probably full of ghosts, too.

His cousin Wendy, three years his junior, waved from the top stoop step. She butted out her cigarette and flicked it past him to the sidewalk. "I win the bet," she said, offering her hand so he could pull her upright.

"You're smoking now? What bet?"

"That you'd show. Dad owes me five bucks. And yeah, as long as I do it outside."

"Glad I could help. And smoking will stunt your growth, Squirt."

"Yeah, yeah, yeah." She glanced at his rucksack. "You got it?"

"Not out here."

"But you got it?"

He grinned briefly, and took her shoulder. "Come on, it's cold and I'm freezing."

They went inside.

Uncle Fred was in the vestibule trying to put the leash on Mack the mutt. "Oh," he said. "You're here."

"Happy to see you too, Uncle Fred."

Mack was, certainly, ducking the leash, jumping on Cy, his big paws reaching his shoulders. Cy took Mack's requisite licks, scratched him behind the ears, then took the leash snap from his uncle and attached it to the dog's collar. "Gotcha," he said.

"Want to walk him?"

Cy shook his head. "I wouldn't want to deprive you the pleasure."

Upstairs, he found his bedroom as he had left it in August. The only changes were fresh vacuum tracks in the carpet, and his aunt had even dusted at some point. She hadn't bet against him, anyway. He heaved his rucksack onto his desk chair, pulled his coat off and dropped it to the floor, then flung himself across his bed. Outside, an ambulance made its way slowly up 6th Avenue. The sound of its siren dredged up bad memories, and caused a thousand little spiders to crawl up his back and into his hair.

"Hey."

He turned over. Wendy stood in the doorway. "Yeah."

"So…"

He gestured to his rucksack with his chin. "It's in there."

She went over to it. "How much?"

"You said you wanted two bags."

"Yeah, so how much?"

He shook his head. "Merry Christmas."

"You're kidding."

"Serious as a heart attack."

She crossed over to him, knelt, and gave him a hug. "Thank you cuz."

"My pleasure. Now get it out of here before your dad finds it and busts my ass."

Aunt Carol couldn't be bothered cooking the night before the big feast, so they got a pizza from Ray's on 7th.

"So." Uncle Fred put down his slice and wiped his mouth

with his napkin. "What is this thing?"

Cy chewed and swallowed before answering. "What thing?"

"This Rooker thing."

"You know about that?"

"We got a letter," Aunt Carol said.

Cy looked at her, then back at his uncle. "It's...just a thing."

"Just a thing? It's a bit more than that, Cyrus."

"It's an award. For a painting I did."

"The letter said your tuition is covered to graduation, and graduate school too."

"If I maintain a 3.0 and get an MFA there, yeah."

"Wow," Wendy said.

Uncle Fred leaned forward. "So what is the painting?"

"A portrait. A full-length portrait. Big one."

"Of who?"

Cy took in a breath through his nose, then let it out. "An angel."

Everyone was silent, staring at him. Cy the atheist, painting angels? He decided, *what the hell:* "It's actually a portrait of a fallen angel, a dark angel, one of the bad guys. Caim."

"Cain?"

"No. Caim. With an 'M'." Cy passed a piece of cheese from his pizza to Mack, under the table.

"So." His uncle moved his plate over an inch. "You're going religious now?"

"No such luck. It's just a painting."

"Of Caim. A fallen angel from Hell. One of the bad guys."

"It's just a painting, Uncle Fred."

They looked at one another across the table.

Aunt Carol leaned over and planted a kiss on Cy's cheek. "Let's just call it a painting that's paying for the rest of Cy's college education, shall we?" She gave his shoulder a little squeeze and shake. "We're so proud of you! Who knew?"

"Wow," Wendy said, again.

His cousin poked her head out of the roof trap door.

"There you are."

The cheap aluminum folding lounger creaked as Cy turned. "I needed the fresh air."

She came all the way up, and closed the trap door with hardly a sound. "I haven't been up here since the summer."

"Here I thought you'd be smoking up a storm up here, like one of these chimneys."

"Too many stairs. So how's the view?"

Cy turned back to the chimneys, vent pipes and television antennas, and the soft evening glitter of the real estate cliff across the river. *All that Upper East Side old and new money over there.* "Same."

She took the folding chair next to him. "We should take these down, you know? The winter will murder them."

"I think that ship has already sailed, Squirt."

She sank her chin into her coat. "I was looking for you after dinner."

"I was on the third floor, looking at some stuff."

"Your old stuff?"

"No. My parents'."

"Oh." She looked at him, then out, across the brownstone roofs. "I never knew them."

"You were just a baby."

"You must still remember them, though."

"Yeah."

She shivered. "We should go back down."

He turned to her; they both heard one of the old nylon straps tear. "Do you believe in ghosts?"

"*What?*"

"Ghosts. Do you believe in them?"

"I don't know." She frowned. "I never thought about it. Do you?"

"Yeah." He lay back again. "Yeah, I do."

"Have you seen one?"

He was quiet for a long moment. "Yeah," he said, finally.

"For real?"

He nodded.

"Where? Not here? Please tell me not here."

"No. At school."

"Seriously?"

He nodded again.

"What was it? Who was it? I mean, did you–"

"It was my mom."

She looked at him in disbelief. "I'm not amused, Cyrus. You're fooling with me, right? Your *mom*?"

He rubbed his eyes. "Where's my Washburn?"

"Your what?"

"My guitar. It isn't in my closet. I looked."

"I...I thought I might try to learn, you know, how to play. When you didn't take it to school with you I thought...."

He got up, stretched. "Keep it," he said.

"Keep it, like, it's mine?"

"Learn how to play it, though. Promise me."

"Sure. I mean, I promise. You mean it for real? You really want me to have it?"

He tousled her hair. "You're right. It's freaking Arctic up here. We should go back down."

Tuesday, December 3, 1974

Cy found a student sitting cross-legged outside Professor Baylor's door. *Shit*, he said to himself, and then, to the student, "Office hours?"

The student looked like he had missed a day or two of sleep. He pushed a greasy length of hair behind his ear. "Yeah. Most of the morning. Listen, I only need ten minutes. Do you mind if I cut ahead of you?"

"I don't have an appointment either. You're here first, so..."

"Baylor's your advisor too?"

"Me? Hell no. I'm at Goddard. Painting major."

"No shit. So you just paint paintings all day?"

"Something like that." Cy sat on his coat and put his rucksack in his lap.

The student pondered the wall opposite them. "Lucky you."

"You're pre-med?"

"For about ten more minutes, anyway."

"Damn. Sorry about that."

The student shrugged. "I'm actually relieved. I can take Baylor yelling. He yells all the time anyway. The hard part will be telling my parents."

The office door beside him opened, and a tall black girl emerged. "He's in one of his moods," she whispered down to them as she passed.

"Great." The soon-to-be-ex pre-med student stood, shoved his hair behind his ears again, and grinned down to Cy before knocking and entering.

"Good luck," Cy said to the closing door.

The muffled conversation through the pebbled glass above him began low, with the student doing most of the talking. Then Professor Baylor's voice rose, and the student's voice rose as well, if briefly. Cy heard the shriek of a chair across the floor, then the door opened abruptly and the student came out, closing the door behind him, not quite, but almost, slamming it. He stood there, panting, staring at his hand on the doorknob for a long moment before finally letting go. "Fuck you too," he said under his breath. Then he saw Cy. "Not you. Him."

Cy couldn't think of anything to say that didn't sound lame, so he remained silent as the student looked left, then right, then shook his head fiercely, his hair flying, and made for the stairwell.

Cy gathered his coat and rucksack as he rose, and entered the professor's office without knocking.

Baylor stood behind his desk, his back to the door. He whirled around at Cy's entrance. "Who–!" His face showed a mix of emotions, then cleared, leaving only recognition. "Mr. Barnaby," he said. "You do not have an appointment."

"No, sir. I was just hoping you had a few minutes for me."

Baylor looked at his Regulator clock on the wall, partially

hidden by the hanging turkey vulture. "I have nothing for you to draw today. Nothing to paint. My next appointment—"

"I just have a question."

Baylor startled at the sound of someone in the hall calling out to someone else. He grabbed for the edge of his desk, blinking rapidly.

Cy said, "Are you okay?"

"Yes, of course." Baylor wiped a hand across his mouth as he took a seat behind his cluttered desk. "Just busy, always busy." He pointed to the chair by the stuffed chimp, the only one clear of books. "Sit, if you must." Bright morning light through his glasses cast jerking rainbows across his hands as he folded and refolded them. "Ask your question."

Cy felt the chimp staring at him as he perched on the edge of the chair. "I just have to know, about the words, the messages."

Baylor's hands came together in a tight knot.

"I need to know if they're real."

"Of course they are real. Are you doubting your eyes?"

"No, that's not what I mean."

More voices in the hall. Baylor looked past Cy. "Your point, Mr. Barnaby."

"The new ones, the ones I did the watercolors for. I need to know if someone, someone somewhere, someone *real*, could have made them happen."

Baylor returned his attention to Cy. "Someone who recently passed, you mean. Crazy old Professor Baylor communicating with dead people."

"That's not what I mean, not at all. The last one I saw, the last one I painted, it said 'Sirius.'"

Baylor had his full attention now. "Perhaps the name of the star. I recall we discussed this point."

"I...knew someone. She sometimes called me that."

"She called you a star?"

"As a joke. Sometimes she thought I was being too serious. Sirius and serious." He spelled both words. "Serious Cyrus."

"And how does this relate to the word spelled out in the caul tissue?"

"Because she *died*, professor. She died when I was just a little kid."

Baylor was silent, expressionless. Then, "You think someone you knew, someone now dead, is speaking to you, specifically to you? Through the cauls? You think a connection in life translates to a connection in death?"

"It's just too close of a coincidence."

"A coincidence, Mr. Barnaby. The correct word. The exact word. They occur. To anyone else this would be nothing more. Just a coincidence."

Cy opened his mouth to reply, but Baylor waved his hand, and took off his glasses as he rose. "Perhaps," he said, with a weary note, "perhaps our work here is done."

"What do you mean?"

Baylor looked at Cy with watery, washed-out eyes. "I fear our arrangement must be finished. We are at an end."

The chair seemed to drop out from under Cy. "Wait. Wait. You're *firing* me?"

"I consider it best. Best for you, certainly."

"Wait!" Cy fought back a sudden surge of helpless anger. "Please. *Please.* You can't. You *can't*..."

Baylor put his glasses back on. "No, young man. It is clearly too important to you. Clearly. Too dangerous. The temptation. No. I must insist." He made shooing motions with his hands, brushing Cy away, dismissing him.

Cy's voice rose almost to a shout: "But you don't understand! This is the only way I can talk to her!"

"Goodbye Mr. Barnaby."

"No! You can't do this!" Sudden tears fell, hot tears, streaking Cy's cheeks. "You can't!"

"And tell your friend, the young lady with so much make-up, to never bother me again."

"Wait. Who?"

Baylor waved his hand in dismissal. "I'm sorry. I truly am."

Cy banged his fist on the desk. "You have to listen to me!"

Baylor skirted his desk, strode to the office door, and opened it. "Leave," he said, all sympathy gone, now. "Leave, or I will call Security."

He walked through the falling snow with his hood up and his hands buried in his coat pockets. Bliss Hall emerged like a hulking gray wraith. Inside, he ignored the protestations of the RA behind the lobby desk, and went upstairs.

He struck Betsy's door with his fist, then burst in.

She had on a long black bathrobe, hair wet, no makeup, like she had just come from the showers. She ran to him and tried to hug him, but he held her at arm's length. "What did you do?"

"What do you mean?"

"Professor Baylor. What the hell did you do?"

"I saw them, Cyrus. I saw them!"

"Saw what?"

"The cauls! The ones he keeps in the refrigerator."

"When?"

"Yesterday! I just barged in, you know? Shoved my tits right in his face. What could he do? I told him I knew about the cauls, told him he had to take me down to the dissection rooms to see them. I gave him total shit, believe me. It was fun. I think I scared the hell out of him. He finally showed me the ones in the fridge in his office. Did you know about them? He's got like dozens of them in there—"

"You ruined it." His voice broke. "You ruined everything!" He pushed her away, turning, but she grabbed him, and pulled him close again. "Stay. Please. Stay with me."

He shook himself free. "I'm going home."

"Cyrus!"

He waved her off, stepped back into the hall, and made for the stairs.

"Don't you dare walk away from me. Cyrus!"

He kept walking.

She stood outside her door. "Cyrus!"

"Leave me alone!" he yelled over his shoulder, avoiding the looks of the other girls, drawn out of their rooms to see what the commotion was about. "Everybody," he muttered to himself, pulling his hood up. "Everybody just leave me alone."

Cy sat in an old ladder back chair, in his studio space, in the basement of Our House. He hadn't turned on the overhead fluorescents, but some light filtered down from the open door at the top of the stairs; it was enough. He looked at the canvas on the easel. He looked without emotion, without…anything. Cows in pre-dawn shadow, wandering up the slope of a field. Cows, grass, sky…vague shapes in the dark. It was only…a painting.

The public phone in the hall upstairs rang, startling him. He looked up. *Don't answer it. Let it go.*

Someone came down from the second floor, though, and caught it on the fifth ring. "Hello?" Kate, her voice muffled through the floor above. "…Just a minute. He might be downstairs." She came down the hall to the basement doorway and called to him in a stage whisper: "Cy? You down there?"

"I'm not home."

"It's the Coffin Lady."

"Then I'm definitely not home."

The floor above creaked as she returned to the phone. "I'm sorry but he's not there… No, I don't, sorry… Yeah, you too." He heard her hang up, then come back to the basement doorway. "You okay?"

"I'm fine."

"You're sitting in the dark."

"I'm thinking."

"She sounded really pissed-off."

"Good for her."

Kate was quiet for a moment. "You sure you're okay?"

"I'm just peachy. Seriously. Thanks for taking care of the call."

"You're welcome." She lingered at the doorway for another moment, then he heard her footsteps go down the hall, and back up the stairs.

He returned his attention to the painting, to the cows still wandering up the hill…to a dawn that would never come.

Before he finally went up to his room he took down the double clothesline strung on hooks by the washer and dryer. He coiled it carefully, and took it with him.

Upstairs, door closed, with only his desk lamp for light, he found an empty page in one of his spiral-bound notebooks, stared at it awhile, then picked up a thin black marker and wrote:

I feel like I'm not supposed to be here. Like everything was a mistake, everything since the car accident, everything since I was five. Like it's not real. Like it wasn't supposed to happen. Being dead, with my parents, dying when they did — THAT is real.

He put down the marker, rubbed his eyes with both hands, wiped away leaking tears, and took some deep breaths. He read over what he had written, blinking, frowning. He ripped the page out, crumpled it into a tight ball, and threw it over his shoulder. He took more deep breaths, blinked away more tears, and then, on a fresh page, wrote two words, big, all capitals, bearing down hard.

He stared at the words for nearly a minute. Then, with care, he tore the page free, and folded it small enough to put in his pocket. He had to stand to do it.

There. *There.*

He took in one more long, deep breath, and as he did so, something, some*one*, touched his shoulder.

He spun around, stifling a cry.

Across the room, in the northwest corner, the crumpled ball of notepaper peeked out around the pumpkin crate of records.

With only the desk lamp for light, he couldn't see how many shadows were there, in that corner, but he knew, *he knew*, there had to be more than one.

A shiver passed through him, and a welcoming, numbing cold.

He opened his arms, and she came to him, hugged him, *cradled him....*

Wednesday, December 4, 1974

Detective Second-Grade Edward Schuyler watched the county coroner's office crew load the body in their van. The assistant medical examiner, a raw-faced thirty-something named Smith, was still in the bubble, looking up at the limb where the clothesline had been tied Schuyler went over. "He must have climbed up there and just jumped," Smith said. "Third and fourth cervical vertebrae completely separated, spinal cord as well, probably. We'll know when we open him up." He looked down to include Schuyler. "A jump like that, twenty more pounds on him, if the clothesline didn't part first he might have ripped his head clean off. '

"That an official finding, Doctor?"

Smith let out his breath. "Sorry. I'm tired. It's been a long day." He glanced at his watch. "Hell, it's already tomorrow."

Schuyler gestured to the large plastic evidence bag stuffed with smaller evidence baggies, all neatly labeled, shoved under Smith's arm. "I'll take those, if you like."

"Oh. Right. Sorry. All from his person." Smith handed the bag to him. "I thought you might want to see this one first, though." He held out a final bag, one of the nine-by-twelves, containing an unfolded piece of college-ruled notepaper.

"Suicide note?"

Smith nodded. "In his left front pants pocket. Short and sweet."

Schuyler took it, angling the bag to catch a flood light. Two words, hand printed in black marker:

He looked up. "Read what? Was there something else on him? Another note?"

Smith shook his head. "Just the usual stuff kids carry." He pointed to the large evidence bag. "It's all in there."

Schuyler read the two words to himself again. "What are we supposed to read, then?"

"Beats me," Smith said.

Thursday, January 9, 1975

Cindy, the new girl, closed and locked her bedroom door, crossed the landing, and paused at Kate's open doorway. Kate, sitting cross-legged on her bed with an open textbook in her lap, looked up, and took the highlighter out of her mouth. "Hey," she said. "Settling in okay?"

"Yeah. I just need to get the rest of my clothes from my dorm and I'll be done. The closet's kind of tiny, though."

"Old house."

"I like old houses, though." Cindy rapped the door jamb with her knuckle. "Especially old haunted ones."

Kate gestured with the highlighter. "There are some extra dressers in the basement. We can ask Ben to help bring one up if you need it."

"I think I'll be okay, thanks. I actually wanted to thank you for the other thing."

"What thing?"

"For doing my dishes last night. I left them in the sink, to do them later? But when I came back they were done."

Kate shook her head slowly. "Wasn't me."

"Maybe it was Brenda. Or Ben. Sort of a "welcome to Our House" kind of thing… Hey, are you okay?"

Kate looked at her, then back down at her textbook "Yeah," she said. "I'm fine."

Ghost
Stories

300 Down

The first painting was still in Arthur's gallery backstock when he stumbled across the second.

Angela, his gallery manager, wrinkled her nose when he showed her. "My God, Arthur! Why on Earth did you buy that?"

He looked at it again. "Honestly? I don't know. It seemed …familiar."

"It should. It looks just like that other horrid little thing you bought a few months ago in Philadelphia. You know, the redhead in the green dress?" She clicked a few keys, swiped her thumb across the touchpad, then swung the screen so he could see. "Bottom row, near the center."

Then he did know. Christ.

He went to the basement backstock, found the painting in the high slots, where all his "maybes" and Angela's "oh my Gods" went after he returned from his buying trips, and pulled it out, into the hard light. "Shit," he said. Angela was right. They were the same painting, or, at least the same subject. Different hair-style, different dress, and she smiled a bit more in the new one. But definitely her. Another crass, brassy redhead in a green dress.

Angela had followed him down. She looked over his shoulder, and clucked. "Told you."

Sally ran a tight ship at her Georgetown gallery, but Arthur had heard the rumor anyway.

She met him at the door. "Back again so soon?"

"What, have I worn out my welcome?"

She gave him one of her signature belly laughs. No sincerity in it, but Arthur appreciated the effort.

"You know yours is the first gallery I visit when I'm in D.C.," he said. "Anyway, I was talking to Sonya a few days ago and she let slip you have an uncatalogued Hopper."

"Sonya has a big mouth." Sally motioned toward the back with her chin. "I have some other new things that might interest you. All offensively expensive, of course." As Arthur passed her she added, "You couldn't afford the Hopper."

"Very funny." Arthur dodged through a small jungle of pedestal sculpture. "I'm after portraits, anyway."

Behind him, following, Sally made an inopportune sound. "Portraits. Who buys portraits these days?"

Arthur stopped, turned. "Me, if it's the right one."

"Wait, didn't you recently purchase one from Aloysius in Philly—?"

"Al is another schmuck with a big mouth."

"Selling Arthur Wakefield a portrait is An Event. Especially an Expressionist one. Word gets around."

"I'm sure. Anyway, it reminded me of something."

"Brilliant orange hair, crazy ice-blue eyes, blood-red lips, neon green dress, yes? Horrid little thing."

"Those were my gallery manager's exact words."

"Angela has taste."

Arthur paused to look at a Linden Frederick, one of his little studies from 2009; he sighed, and dismissed it. "He charged me enough for it as I recall."

Sally sniffed. "That one you could afford. Unlike...this."

They had stopped before the Hopper. It was one of his New York street scenes from the late 1920s. A prospective buyer came instantly to mind.

"Purchased from the original owner's family," Sally said. "It hung in her bedroom in Chelsea since the day she bought it in 1928. Never catalogued, never shown."

"How much are you asking?"

"Ah. Well."

"How *much*?"

Sally murmured a figure.

Arthur gave her another.

Sally blinked. "Jesus. You have actually surprised me." She stuck out her hand. "Sold." She regarded him. "You make me wish I had a portrait of a redhead in a green dress to sell."

"Do you?"

Sally shook her head. "But if I ever do, you're the first schmuck I'm calling."

Arthur entered the evening crowd on N Street like a fish in rapids, jostled along by the occasional bump or push as everyone headed for that after-work drink, or the Metro home. Just before reaching 34th someone connected hard, shoulder-to-shoulder, and he staggered to keep his feet as he swung about. "Hey—!" he began, a rock in the river now, parting rapids, as the person who had struck him—a woman, red-haired, with a triumphant grin splitting her scarlet slash of a mouth—lost herself in the crowd. Beneath her coat, before she was totally gone: a flash of lurid green.

Then he remembered. Suddenly, like a screen switched on, flooding his brain with glaring images, he remembered.

"Marie!" But that was impossible, of course. Marie was dead. She was as dead as dead could be, and had been for twenty, no, twenty-*one* years.

Marie was dead.

A week later, returning from lunch, Angela saw the two paintings, neatly wrapped and leaning by the alley door. "It's starting to snow," she informed Arthur as she passed his open office door. Coat hung, on her way back, she asked, "Taking a few home?"

He looked up from his laptop. "The transport company took the big Stella from my apartment last night. The Chinese buyer is in a big hurry apparently." He returned his attention to the screen. "Freed up space on a wall."

"That's nice. So which ones are you taking? I'll make the entries."

He looked up again. "What?"

"Which two are you taking home? I'm assuming you haven't noted it in the database."

"Actually, I did."

Her expression was deadpan. "You're serious."

"As a heart attack."

"The Stella pickup too?"

He smiled at her briefly, then returned to his work.

Five minutes later she was back at his doorway. "I can*not* believe you are taking those two ugly little redhead portraits home with you."

He spread his hands. "They've grown on me. We've had zero client interest, and anyway, you hate them."

"But..." She held a finger up, pointing at nothing and nowhere. "Wasn't that Stella in your bedroom?"

"Took up the entire north wall."

"So...these two are going into your bedroom."

He nodded. Before she could turn he asked, "How many inches?"

"How many inches what?"

"The snow. How deep?"

She shook her head as though to clear it. "They're expecting two or three."

"Lovely." He turned back to his laptop, "Snowfall in the city," and punched a key. "Just glad I don't have to drive in it."

Two of the three ceiling accent lights he had positioned for the big Stella protractor series piece were perfectly placed for the two portraits. Arthur sat at the end of his bed, gazing at them.

The two redheads with their arresting blue eyes, red-slashed mouths and loud green dresses looked brazenly back at him.

"You're not her," he said, into the empty air. "You're not Marie."

Their smiles, each different, each distinct, shared one thing: they sneered.

He got up, went to the painting on the left, the more recently painted of the two ("That's the other thing," Angela had complained, "It's anonymous *and* new; nobody buys new-anonymous, Arthur.") and adjusted its level slightly. "You don't even really look like her," he said.

He crossed the sea of carpet to the patio doors and looked out. "Three inches my ass." The wind whipped across the wide expanse of glass, carrying curtains of snow on its shoulders. Below, three hundred feet down, children from the lower floor condos were probably trying to build snowmen in the courtyard.

("You can relax, Arthur," his attorney had told him, two decades ago. "The medical examiner has ruled it an accidental death. If she didn't jump she slipped, she fell, end of story. The district attorney has nothing, now. You're in the clear.")

He turned. "She slipped," he informed the portraits on the wall. "She fell. I'm innocent."

They sneered back at him.

"You have a visitor." Angela handed him his coffee as he passed her the next day. "In the conference room."

He stopped. "A visitor."

"In the conference room."

"Is this a game? Do I get three questions?"

"It's your wife."

Arthur paused his coffee halfway to his mouth. "My ex-wife."

Angela let out a long, calming breath. "Your ex-wife is in the conference room."

"Why didn't you put her in my office?"

"Because the last time I did that, you complained she

'fiddled' with your things. And anyway, she specifically asked for the conference room."

"Wonderful," he said.

The conference room was at the end of the short hall. He stopped in the doorway, testing a smile. "Sylvia! I'd offer you coffee, but I'm sure you're in a hurry."

Her returned smile was equally false. "I've sold the Amagansett house."

"Really." He took a seat opposite her. "I always thought you loved that place."

"I do, but I'm spending most of my time on the coast now. It just sits empty, even during the season."

"A pity. I always liked it."

Her false smile flashed again. "You hated it. Sand in the carpet. The penthouse here in town is more your style, anyway."

She was right, of course. The east-side penthouse had been his before the marriage, and he had made damn sure it was still his after. "So…you came to tell me you sold the house out east. You could have emailed, texted, *phoned*…"

"Actually, I came in person to give you this." She reached under the table and lifted a flat rectangular package, a bit larger than one by two, and slid it across to him.

"A late Christmas present? I'm touched."

"I found it when the movers were packing." Her well-manicured nail tapped the brown paper wrapping. "There's no way in hell this was going to Santa Barbara with me."

He picked the package up. "If I remember the gory details of the settlement, you got both houses *and* all the contents in them."

"Not this." Her voice was flat, but her eyes flashed in sudden anger. "I don't want it, but I thought you might."

He began worrying at the packing tape. "You've got me curious. Should I open it now?"

"God no." She rose, and remembered perfume wafted across the table. "Wait till after I'm gone, please." She extended a hand. "If you're ever on the coast…"

He gave it a weak squeeze. "Always a pleasure, darling."

She gave the package a final venomous glare, then skirted the table for the door. "I'll see myself out. I hope you enjoy…it."

Angela appeared at the conference room door a few minutes later. "Don't forget your ten-o'clock," she said. Then, "She gave you a painting?"

He stood it up in one of the chairs.

"Oh my God," she said, "not another one!"

A young woman in three-quarter view stared defiantly out of the canvas, a blue-eyed, scarlet-lipsticked redhead in a green dress.

"This one's different," he said.

"Well, smaller, but—"

"No. That's not it. I know who painted this one, and I know when. She was a young artist, fresh out of Cooper-Union. Her name was Maria Millard."

Angela shook her head slowly. "Not ringing any bells."

"She was before your time. She brought a portfolio to show me, hoping for representation, over twenty years ago. I…ended up not taking her on."

"Because she only painted redheads in green dresses?"

"Well, she did do this one, but she didn't do the other two."

Angela inspected it closely. "The color and style are the same, even the brushstroke. This Maria Millard of yours must have done them all."

"Impossible. The other two are relatively recent, five, ten years old. Agreed?"

She nodded, her expression wary. "So?"

"So very shortly after Maria Millard painted this one, twenty-one years ago, she died. Slipped and fell." He turned away slightly. "Off a penthouse patio."

"But—" Then realization dawned on her, and she put her hand to her lips. "Oh *Arthur*…" She made a motion to go to him, but he raised his hand. "It's old news," he said.

"So your wife—"

"Ex-wife."

"So your ex-wife had it and just now decided to give it back to you?"

"Sylvia didn't know about it. She knew about her, about Maria, but not the self-portrait. The movers, packing things up, must have unearthed it." He let his breath out. "She's selling the Amagansett house."

"Did you just say self-portrait?"

"Her hair was more auburn than red. And she rarely wore lipstick, never bright red. And as for the dress...paint-stained jeans and tee shirts were more her style."

Angela looked at him, letting a few moments pass. Then, "Are you okay?"

He turned back to the painting. "I'm fine." He stood there for a long moment before rousing himself. "Reschedule the ten-o'clock." He picked the painting off the chair. "I'm taking this home."

His building was only three blocks east. It was snowing again, new snow over old. The pedestrian traffic was heavy, and the mix at this time of morning was about fifty-fifty commuter and tourist. Arthur found himself at the front of the crowd at the corner with Third. Contractor vans and taxis crowded the avenue, barreling south. He had put the little painting in a leather portfolio case, safe from the weather, and he held it securely under his arm, waiting with the unwashed masses for the light to change.

The shove came right between his shoulder blades, perfectly placed to push him completely off-balance. In that moment as he fell into the slushy gutter he saw two things, distinct and clear: the first was the woman who had pushed him, with bright red hair twirling about her shoulders as she worked herself back into the crowd...and the second was the oncoming taxi in the right-hand lane, accelerating through the intersection to beat the light.

I'm dead, he thought, at the end of that moment, closing his eyes as he fell heavily to the pavement, directly in the path of the oncoming taxi. *She did it. I'm dead.*

A screech of brakes combined with the sudden screams of people.

No contact. No hit. He opened his eyes, and saw the underside of a filthy bumper, dripping grey slush in his face. *Oh God.* The taxi had stopped in time. *Dear God.*

The next few minutes were a blur of being pulled out from under by helping hands, voices yelling: "Don't move him!" and others: "The taxi didn't touch him!" and "I'm fine, really, I'm fine," realizing that was *his* voice, babbling as he was led to the curb, leaning against a pole, holding the painting—the portfolio case not mangled or torn, just wet and scraped a bit—tight against him. When he heard someone say they had called 911 he straightened, and steadied himself against the pole. Oh no; no police; no questions. No *way.* He shook off all remaining offers of help. "Really," he said, "I'm okay. I'm fine." Looking over his shoulder more than once, he crossed the avenue like a retreating soldier, with the light.

He took a long scalding shower, put on warm and comfortable clothes, and got the gas fireplace in the living room lit. Somehow, though, it wasn't enough to take off the chill he still felt inside. He raised the thermostat, and put on a sweater, but he still found himself shivering.

He startled when the phone in his pocket rang. He pulled it out, stared at Angela's name on the screen, but still let it go five more rings before answering.

"So," she said, "where are you? Still home?"

"I have a good reason." He told her what had happened at the intersection, but left out the push. "I slipped," he said. "The curb was…icy."

"Holy crap Arthur! Are you all right?"

"My shoulder hurts like hell, but I'll be fine. Probably just a bruise. I saved the painting anyway."

"Who gives a damn about that horrible little painting? As long as you're okay…"

"I'll be fine." He looked across the room at the portfolio case leaning up against the fireplace hearth ledge. "Good as new by tomorrow."

"Well you only have the one-o'clock scheduled for the afternoon anyway, with Harvey."

"Harvey can wait."

"Take a hot shower."

"Already did."

"Get that fireplace going."

"Crackling as we speak."

"Watch an old movie on that monster TV of yours. *Relax.*"

"On the agenda. Jimmy Stewart, I think. See you tomorrow."

He thumbed the phone, and dropped it back in his pocket. When he stood, the pain in his right shoulder was bright, but bearable. He crossed to the fireplace, took up the portfolio, and brought it into his bedroom. When he unzipped and opened it, he couldn't decide if he felt relieved or disappointed that the painting inside was untouched.

"You bitch," he said to the leering redhead. "You tried to kill me. You *bitch.*"

He picked the painting up, and a sudden desire to slam the canvas down on the nearby bedpost washed over him in a hot wave. Up close, the blue eyes had laughter in them, the same laughter he could see in the other two.

She knew. They all did.

The new painting needed wiring and framing, but he just hung it on the wall bracket by the top stretcher bar. The alignment with the ceiling accent light wasn't ideal, but with his shoulder there was no way he could move the light. It would do.

He stood back. There, all three paintings, side by side by side.

"Fuck you," he said softly. "And you, and you."

His shoulder throbbed, and twisting his neck only prompted the beginnings of a headache. His choices were either the leftover pills from his summer ankle sprain, or the remaining two inches of his favorite single malt. He chose the scotch. And after that…

He awoke from his nap to someone knocking at the apartment door. He heard three knocks in steady succession, a momentary pause, then one more. He rolled onto his good side, favoring his shoulder, burying his face in the pillow. There was a perfectly good doorbell. Why didn't they—?

Four more knocks, in the same pattern as the first time. Not loud either, not insistent. They were calm. Measured. Knock-knock-knock…*knock*.

Afternoon sunlight slanted across the bedroom. The snow was over. He squinted through the glare to his bedside clock. Two forty-three. Who the hell—?

Then a thin, crystal stiletto blade of fear pierced his chest, and for a moment he couldn't breathe. Oh my God, he thought, gasping, blinking in the light. He remembered the knock, the pattern. It had been *her* knock; *her* pattern.

Silence. He waited for more knocks, but none came. The silence lengthened.

He sat up slowly, realizing as he did so that he was shaking, and panting like a frightened dog. The portraits looked at him from the wall. Still leering, still laughing at him.

He eased out of bed and stood for a moment, listening, then went into the hallway, to his wide, deep living room. The silence lengthened further. The front door of his apartment was down the other short hallway, just out of sight from where he stood. The kitchen was that way as well, with the service door tucked away in the utility room beyond.

The service door.

He went quickly through the living room, shielding his eyes from the sun-glare off the patio snow, then through the kitchen to the utility room: washer, dryer, sink, folding table, closet…and the service door. He could take the fire stairs down to the next floor, then the elevator to the lobby. Then he could—

Knock, knock, knock…knock.

He staggered back, grabbing blindly. She was on the other

side of this door now!

Knock, knock, knock...knock.

He ran back through the kitchen, into the entry hall to the living room. Behind him, from the front door:

Knock, knock, knock...knock.

The only other way out was the patio, the railing, and a drop to the courtyard.

He ran, stumbling, across the living room to the patio doors, fumbled with the locks, ignoring his shoulder as he wrenched the doors open. The cold air slapped him in the face, the snow like fire on his feet as he plowed across the patio to the railing. He grabbed it, flinging snow off to get a better grip, and looked down.

Where, in the courtyard far below, the redhead in a green dress looked back up at him.

It's for You

The first to die was Detective Sergeant George Small, re-tired, formerly of the Homicide Unit. At home, said Widow Small; quietly, in his own bed.

Frank picked up the manila envelope from his desk pile, hefted it, felt the contents shift. "What's this?"

"Flowers for Mrs. Small," Detective Mike Finnean said. "Five buck minimum."

"Jesus." Frank blinked. "They're dropping like flies these days."

His partner nodded slowly. "They say it always goes down in threes, Frankie."

"Better write your will then, Mike. You don't look so good." Frank made his contribution, then waved the envelope over his head. "Who's next?"

"Over here." That was Jack Hyde, an old friend and former partner of Small's, as he leaned forward to take a phone call.

Frank was about to do a Frisbee toss with the envelope when the duty sergeant with the game leg raised his voice over the general clamor of the squad room: "Phone for you too, Detective Graham!"

"Who is it?"

"Your daughter Julie."

Frank cleared a pile of paper so he could see his phone,

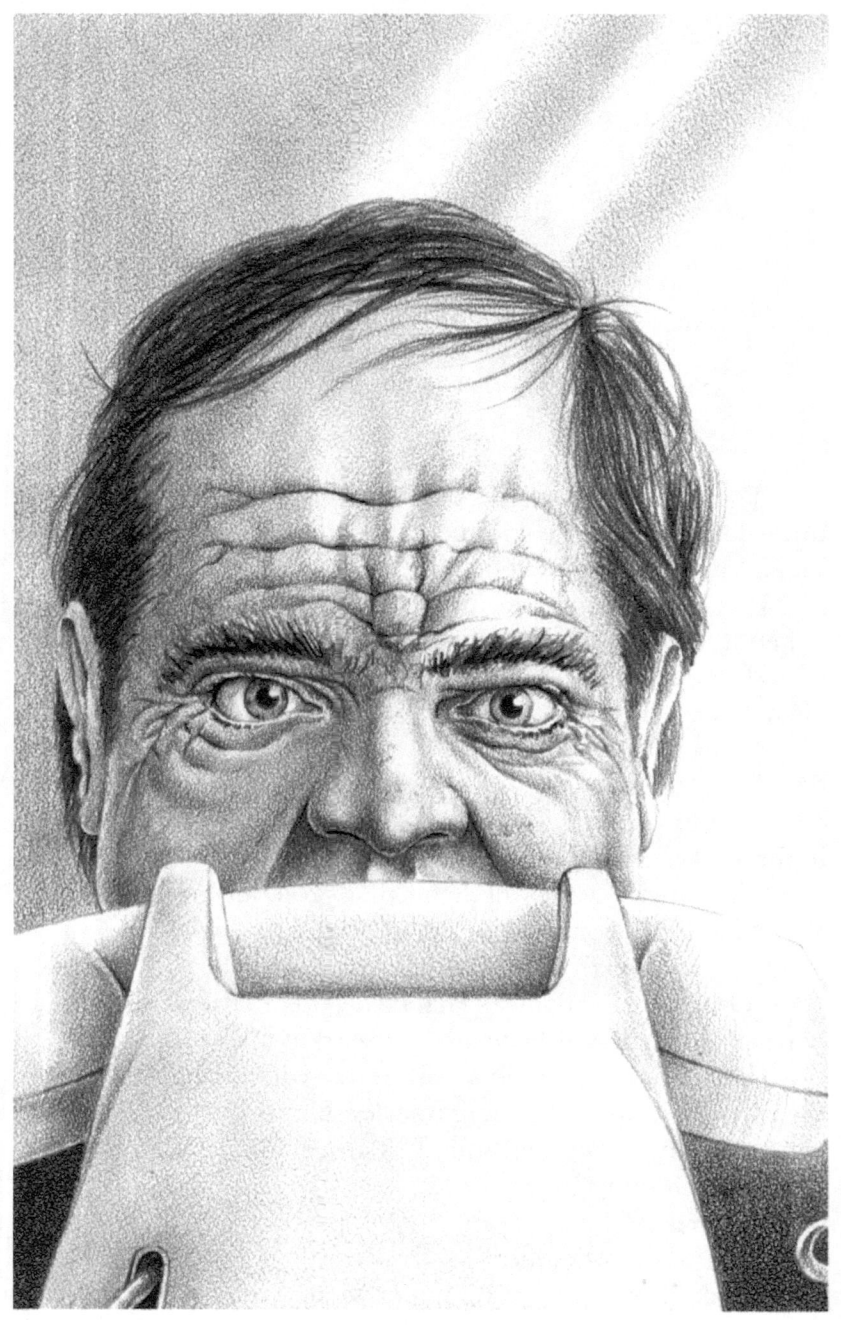

depressed the blinking button light, then leaned his considerable bulk into the swivel chair and buried the receiver in his ear. "What's up, sweet pea?"

"You're on your own for dinner, Pops."

Frank grinned. "What, another date with Donald?"

"Ronald, with an 'R.' Hey, he's buying."

"I hear you. I'll be okay. Tell Donald I said hi."

"*Daad.*"

Snickering, he punched the button light off to break the connection. Across the room, then, he saw that Jack Hyde was still on the phone. "Heads up, Jacky!" He tossed the Small Memorial Fund envelope across the desks and scored a perfect hit in Hyde's 'in' basket.

The other detective didn't move.

"Jack! Hey, buddy, you sleeping?"

The squad room skipped a beat—a moment of odd silence as everyone focused on Hyde. Then the duty sergeant, who had an angle on Hyde's face, uttered a low exclamation, and lurched to his feet.

Frank met him at Hyde's desk. Together, they crouched to the eye level of the seated detective. Hyde stared back at them with glazed eyes. "He's dead," the sergeant said, incredulous, turning to Frank. "ain't he? Dead?"

Hyde held the phone to his ear, his elbow propped between the desk edge and the chair armrest. Afternoon light from the bank of windows over Pine Street reflected in his unblinking gaze. He looked upset to Frank, like he had just received bad news. But yeah, he was dead all right.

By now, the rest of the dicks and support staff of the Homicide Unit were crowded around. Mike Finnean closed Hyde's eyes, took the phone out of his still warm hand—

"Wait." Frank reached out, "Don't—"

—And hung it up. "Shit," he said then, "I probably should have checked to see if someone was still on the line."

Frank frowned up at his partner. "That would have been smart, Mikey, yeah."

"There wasn't anybody," the duty sergeant said, "his button light was out."

Finnean looked around. "Anybody call the goddamn M.E yet?"

One of the younger guys said, "I just saw him down the hall," and broke out of the crowd to get him.

"Must have been his heart," someone said.

Frank rose, feeling his knees crack, conscious, suddenly, of his own heart pounding behind his ribcage. "Of all people: Hyde."

He was Number Two.

An hour later, a shadow crossed Frank's desk. He looked up. The duty sergeant stood there. "I saw how pissed you were when Detective Finnean hung up Hyde's phone," he said, "So I got a copy of the ISDN log." He laid a computer printout, roughly ripped, in the center of the desk clutter.

Frank glanced across the room to the dead detective's empty desk, then picked up the sheet and studied it. "This last call is from Fishtown," he said, matching the exchange to one of the older sections of the city, once Italian, then Black, then Asian, now...God-only knew. "Two-hundred American Street." He looked up. "That sound familiar to you?"

"Nope. Might have been a songbird, you know? Hyde had a pretty good network going for the drug snuffs up there."

Frank nodded. "Did you call it?"

"The number?" The sergeant straightened. "Disconnected, computer voice saying 'the number you have dialed is no longer in service.' Dead end."

"Typical. Hey, thanks anyway." Frank focused on the number on the printout, memorizing it without even thinking. Then he looked across the room again to the empty desk–two deaths in one day; *Jesus*–and slowly shook his head.

It took another day for Number Three.

Finnean turned onto Broad Street into the clogged traffic

and slapped the steering wheel. "When are they gonna finish fixing this fucking street?"

"I'm in no hurry to get back." Frank squinted through the windshield at the jam of cars. "The air conditioning was on the fritz when we left, remember? The squad room must be a goddamn oven by now." He leaned forward, put his hand over one of the dashboard vents. "Speaking of which…."

Finnean reached down and twisted a knob; a loud ratcheting sound issued from somewhere under the dash, then the smell of burning rubber.

"That's enough of that!" Frank turned the knob back to vent fresh, sweltering, monoxide-laced August city air into the car. "So we bake," he said, settling back resignedly.

They crept a block, then Finnean said, "You heard about Kopelman?"

"Augie?" Frank screwed up his face. "Isn't he living in South Carolina, some golf course retirement set-up?"

"'Living' is no longer the operative word, my friend."

"Oh Christ. Dead?"

"Stroke. Fifteenth Tee."

"Shit." Frank conjured the old cop's face in his memory. He had been gone for years, but Frank clearly remembered his loud bark of a laugh, the rancid stink of his cheap cigars… "It always goes in threes," he said, "remember?"

Finnean chuckled hollowly. "Amen to that."

Another block, then Frank said, "I worked with him once."

"Who, Augie? How old were you, twelve?"

"I was less than a year out, wise guy, same as you, riding shotgun in his prowler one night, covering for his partner Billy Palmer out with the flu or some such shit. Back when they painted the prowlers red, remember? He wouldn't let me drive. We were what, twenty-two?"

"Maybe you were. I had that detour through the Army first, my friend."

Frank shook his head. "It's still so weird."

"What, Augie Kopelman cashing in his chips on a golf

course? There are worse ways to go."

"Not just him: all of them, all three. It's just too many dying at once. Three in just a couple of days, think about that."

"Augie was in his seventies easy—"

"But Jack Hyde was only a few years older than us, wasn't he?"

Finnean nodded, staring straight ahead. "He was just sixty-three."

Frank sweated for a long block, then he said, "So how did you find out about Augie?"

"Friend of the Lieutenant's down in Myrtle Beach saw the obit in the paper and made some calls. 'Died with his wedge and his cell phone in his hand,' he said."

"Cell phone? He died on the *phone*?"

"Yeah." Finnean gripped the wheel with both hands, looking for an opportunity to change lanes. "Just like Jack."

The voice on the other end wavered, but had an under-current of steel: an old cop's wife, maybe, but a cop's wife, just the same.

"I don't want to disturb your day, Mrs. Small," Frank said, easing back in his chair, "but I had just a few questions, if you don't mind. About your husband, about…how he died."

"Of course, Detective."

"So you're okay with this?"

"I know the drill." He heard her dentures click. "You just fire away."

Frank flipped his notebook to a clean page. "Was he asleep when it happened?"

"Well, he was in bed, and it was quite late."

"Were you…I mean, was he…I mean—"

She chuckled. "Were we together in bed, do you mean? No. I was in the kitchen. I have this terrible insomnia, you see, and I do the Times crossword in the kitchen, sometimes till two or three in the morning."

"Is that when you discovered your husband, then? At two or

three in the morning?"

"Why, no. Actually, it was only a few minutes after the phone rang that I went in to see who George was talking to."

Frank suddenly felt cold. "There was a phone call?"

"Yes. Your poor wife must be as used to it as I am, all those calls, usually so late."

"Actually, I'm not married at present."

"Divorced? I don't wonder. I'm surprised I lasted as long as I did."

"You said the phone rang…"

"Yes, it rang twice. I assumed that George got it, because it only went two rings."

"And then you went into the bedroom?"

"After a few minutes, yes." She paused. "That was when I found him."

"Do you remember, Mrs. Small, if the phone was hung up?"

"That's funny you should ask, Detective."

"Why so?"

"Because now that I remember, the phone was off the hook, lying on the floor next to the bed. It was making that awful beeping they do, you know? So I hung it up just before I called 911." She paused, then said, "I wonder…"

"Wonder what, Mrs. Small?"

"George was getting a lot of phone calls from someone lately."

"Someone?"

"I could tell they bothered him, those phone calls, but he wouldn't talk about it."

"He never told you who was making the calls?"

"He didn't, no. But the caller did, the one time I picked up the phone and it was him. 'Tell George it's Jimmy,' he said."

Jimmy. Frank took a shallow breath. "You've been a big help, Mrs. Small."

"Well I don't see how I could–"

"Really. Thank you." Frank hung up. He looked at the

phone. Then he shuddered, and pushed it away.

Frank tented his fingers over a full plate of lasagna. "I have a riddle for you."

His daughter Julie frowned. "I'm no good at riddles. I can never figure them out. Pass the bread, will you?"

"Then you'll hate this one," Frank said, handing the basket over, "because it doesn't have an answer. Not yet, anyway."

Her frown deepened. "Is this about work?"

"Maybe." Frank put down his fork. "Now listen: there are these three guys, they each get a phone call, then they die."

"On the phone?"

"Yeah."

"At the same time?"

"No, separate times, separate places."

"Easy. An electrical surge through the phone lines. Phones work on electricity, don't they?"

"They do, but it's not enough to shock you. No, that's not it."

Julie shrugged. "Coincidence, then." She took a bite and chewed slowly; Frank saw the wheels turning, though. "I need more clues," she said then.

"Okay: the phone that the caller used in one of them?"

"Yeah?"

"It was out of service."

"What about the other two?"

"I'm checking. But one phone call was definitely from a line that was officially disconnected."

"Wow." She blinked. "Spooky. So you think the three calls might be related?"

Frank nodded.

Julie laughed outright. "That's crazy, right?"

"That's why it's a riddle."

"See that signpost up ahead, Pop?" She laughed again. "You're in the *Twilight Zone!*"

The temp with the tight ass and even tighter jeans dropped the inter-office folder on Frank's desk, then sashayed out of the squad room with all eyes watching.

"Who the hell does she work for?" someone asked.

"We don't have a 'need to know,'" someone else replied.

Less than a minute later Frank entered the squad room from the general direction of the john. He spied the yellow folder immediately, saw who it was from, and grabbed it up even before his ass hit the chair. He undid the string and pulled out a flimsy blue sheet with perforations running down both sides: the phone records for one Detective Sergeant George Small, recently deceased.

There, towards the bottom, just before the outgoing call to 911...an incoming call from the Fishtown exchange, from Two Hundred American Street. He placed the blue flimsy next to the fax he had received an hour before from the Myrtle Beach PD, a copy of a similar blue flimsy of the cell phone account of one August Kopelman, also recently deceased. The last incoming call on the fax was the same: Fishtown exchange, Two Hundred American Street.

Frank looked at the flimsy and the fax for a long time, trying to believe what his mind was telling him. Three calls from the same address to three cops. Each of them died during the call. Three phone calls, all from Two Hundred American Street. All from a phone number that, as far as the phone company was concerned, was not in service.

He got up, finally, and made his way across the squad room to the duty sergeant's desk. The grease-penciled roster was on the wall behind him. According to the roster, Mike Finnean had a court appearance this morning, and his name was written in red. "Red me out, Joe," Frank said to the sergeant.

The sergeant rose to do the honors. "Where to, Detective?"

"City Hall, Office of Deeds. Then Fishtown."

American Street was a short block of narrow, tired bungalows, with postage-stamp front lawns and sidewalks that were cracked and tilted from trees long since cut down. Every one of the houses needed paint; three were boarded up; one was burned out. It was a sad, lost little street in a section of the city that had last seen prosperity when people wore 'I Like Ike' buttons and parked Studebakers and Ramblers at the curb, one to a family.

Number Two Hundred, no surprise, was one of the three boarded up houses. White clapboard, low-hipped roof; no second floor to speak of. The little lawn was full of waist-high weeds and rusting and rotting trash. Frank dismissed the nailed-shut front door and porch windows, and followed the side alley to the rear. There he found a plywood bulkhead door to the basement, its lock rusted shut. He gave the lock a sharp yank, and the entire hasp broke free of the rotted wood and came loose in his hand. Grunting, he pushed the bulkhead door up and over, letting light spill down the concrete steps. Lots of spider webs, with darkness and silence beyond.

Frank took a step down the stairs, then noticed a neighbor in the next yard, an old woman in a grey housedress, standing in her back door. He pulled out his shield and held it up so the light caught it. "I'm a policeman."

"I know what you are," she shot back. "I'm just watching you; no harm in that, is there?"

"Anybody live here?"

"You mean in that house you're breaking into?"

Frank waited impassively.

The old woman shook her head finally. "Just those drug addict kids, passing through. Not a real person. Not a family. Not for years."

"Were you around when Jimmy Truewell lived here?"

"Truewell!" She put her hands on her bony hips. "That takes me back. He shot that cop, right here, thirty years ago. Right here. 1963. Thirty-*six* years ago. He still in prison?"

"Thank you for your time, ma'am." Frank started again down the basement steps.

The old woman called after him, a sudden anxious note in

her voice: "He didn't get *out*, did he?"

Frank paused. "No ma'am. He didn't get out."

The first floor looked indeed like a succession of addicts and derelicts had made it a home over the years. But Frank was only looking for one thing, and he found it in the short hall between the living room and the kitchen: the telephone jack. It was round with three socket holes, made out of porcelain, originally mounted on the baseboard, but now hanging free by just one grimy black wire. There was no phone in sight. He found another broken jack in the first-floor front bedroom, but again, no phone, nor any way to successfully plug one in.

In the hall, again, walking from the back bedroom to the front of the house, he heard a sound behind him, a sound he hadn't heard for a decade or so, except in old movies: a rotary phone, dialing.

He whirled around, gun out, finger on the trigger guard, legs automatically braced to squeeze one off....

There in the shadow of the hall, back against the wall, there, for just a moment, just a moment, he thought he saw a young man in a loud short-sleeve shirt, sitting on a chair by a little table, a phone cradled against his shoulder, big shit-eating grin on his acne-scarred face....

Then another sound: a car door slamming, out front, and in a brief moment of distraction Frank blinked, and the hallway before him was empty once more. Just the dust, the shadows, the broken porcelain phone jack hanging from its wire. "Fuck me," Frank whispered, easing his stance, raising the gun's muzzle, "Fuck *me*," then slowly re-holstering it.

"Frank." Mike Finnean stood in the kitchen doorway, dressed in his best suit.

"I thought you were in court," Frank said, feeling like he'd been caught at something, and knowing he looked it.

Finnean glanced at Frank's hand still in his coat, still holding the gun-grip, then back up. "Shithead pleaded out. How come you're here?"

"This is where the phone calls came from, Mike, from this house." Frank gestured to the phone jack hanging from the hole in the wall. "But I don't see how."

His partner was silent, watching him. Then he said, "The call to Jack Hyde, you mean?"

"And to George Small. And Augie Kopelman."

Finnean shook his head slowly. "You've been busy, Frankie."

"I went to City Hall first, checked the deed on this place," Frank continued. "Right now the bank owns it, but back in 1963 a man named Truewell lived here."

"Jimmy Truewell." Finnean turned his head briefly to hawk into the hall. "That's right. Pimple-faced little cocksucking piece of shit named Jimmy Truewell."

"Finding that name in all this was a real shot, Mike. Jimmy Truewell. That really jogged my memory, took me back, you know?"

"He killed Augie's partner Billy Palmer that night," Finnean said, looking about. "Right here, in this room. Killed a cop stone cold, and all the state gave him for it was life."

Frank took in a measured breath. "There was Billy Palmer, yeah, there was Jack Hyde, and George Small, and Augie Kopelman...and *you*, Mike, right? All of you, there that night."

"His drug-addict girlfriend called it in, said he had a gun, said he was threatening her with it. We had two units here in minutes." Finnean pointed down the hall to the front of the house, to the front door. "George was on a beat and showed up just as we were going in. It was dark. Truewell had turned all the goddamn lights off. His girlfriend wasn't even here." Finnean went past Frank to the living room, looking about. "There was a lot of confusion in here, five of us, one of him, not a lot of room in here, you know? Somehow he got George's piece, then put one into Billy before we could get him down."

"I remember," Frank said, nodding, "that's how it played out at the trial."

"It could have been any of us, took that slug."

"I know."

"We should have fried the bastard, Frankie. We should have cooked his fucking brains to soup. But no, instead he gets three free squares at Holmesburg every fucking day for the rest of his sorry little cocksucking life."

"Not any more, Mike."

Finnean turned sharply, looked at him, suddenly focused. "He can't be *out*–"

Frank shook his head. "Correctional Medical Facility. Coma. From a stroke."

"Who'd you talk to?"

"Grayson, in the Warden's Office. Said Truewell had it in his cell. By the time they got him some attention he was already out of it."

Finnean grabbed his arm. "*When?*"

"The day before George took his phone call." *Before the first of them died*, Frank wanted to add, but didn't. He searched his partner's face. "Coincidence?"

"Yeah." Finnean let go, turned away. "Coincidence. Must be."

"Somebody sent three good cops to their deaths, Mike."

"That's bullshit, Frankie."

"That somebody? He called them in from *here*." Frank kicked at the broken phone jack. "From *here*, Mike."

"That's fucking bullshit and you know it–"

The questions came out before he could stop them: "Somebody calling in their marker, Mike? Somebody finally getting even?"

Finnean swung about, stepped up into Frank's face; his voice dropped, low, cold: "What are you saying, partner? You saying something *happened?*"

"You tell me, Mike. You were in here. You were with them."

"You're damn straight I was here! I was dodging bullets with the rest of them! I know what went down!"

"Did he call you from prison too, Mike? Like he called George and Augie and Jack? He called you guys a lot just before that stroke, didn't he?"

"You're a fucking nut case, Frankie. He never—"

"George Small: dead. Jack Hyde: dead. Augie Kopelman: dead. They were all here, and now they're all dead." Frank wanted to grab his partner's suit lapels and shake him. "What about you, Mike? What about you, now?"

Finnean's eyes followed his voice: cold, dead. "You weren't there, Frank," he said, now in just a rough whisper, "You weren't there." Then he turned, and disappeared back down the hall to the kitchen. Frank heard him rattle down the basement stairs. Then, after a moment, his partner's car roared to life in the street, then was gone.

"That went well." Frank raised his hands, then dropped them to his sides. "Oh yeah, that went *real* well."

The next day Mike Finnean called in sick. Then the day after that, as well. He had it on the books; no one, not even the Lieutenant, raised an eyebrow. And Frank left him alone, left the folder with the phone records on the corner of his desk, away from the rest of the clutter, unopened, untouched, but there, in plain view.

When he saw the duty sergeant leave his partner's name in red for the third day, however, he decided to make the call. After a few moments, he slammed the receiver down. "Damn!" Then he rose, grabbed his suit coat, and slung it over his shoulder. "Red me out, Joe."

The duty sergeant chuckled. "You got his answering machine too?"

"Yeah."

"So where to?"

"The CMF at Holmsburg."

The duty doctor didn't even offer to accompany him onto the ward. "Truewell, J.? Number Five," he said, hitting the door-lock button, "left side."

"Thanks." Frank went for the door handle.

"Detective."

Frank stopped, turned.

"He's still comatose. He's probably not even going to know you're here."

"I might get lucky. He might come out of it—" Frank snapped his fingers "—like in the movies, you know?"

"Sure." The doctor nodded sagely. "Right."

Frank entered the ward: long, painted light blue, windows down the left side, a nurse station on the right. He nodded to the RN behind the counter, who lowered his newspaper and peered at him over black-rimmed glasses. "Yeah?"

"I'm here to see Truewell," Frank said.

The nurse pointed to the fifth bed with a meaty, hairy fist, then returned to his paper.

Frank found an old man in Number Five, small, thin to emaciation; his pale, deeply wrinkled skin littered with veins, liver spots, and ancient acne scars. He lay on his back, blanket up to his armpits, hands crossed. On one finger, Frank saw a small plastic cap with wires attached to a heart/bp monitoring device hanging off the headboard; on the other wrist, a catheter attached to a IV drip bag. Frank also saw leg restraints attached to the bed frame, going up under the blankets.

His eyes were half-open. That brought Frank up short for a moment, until he saw that the gaze was unwavering and unfocused; he knew most people died with their eyes open, that you had to close them with your fingers—sometimes more than once—to keep them there. Maybe...? But no, the beeps from the machine beside the bed were regular, and the green spikes on the little screen went by like waves at the beach.

Jimmy Truewell looked out the frosted Plexiglas window, looking into the light, motionless, seeing nothing at all, but alive. His eyes were bloodshot, his mouth open far enough to reveal yellowed, peg-like teeth. A thin thread of drool fell from a corner of his cracked, grey lips to the blue paper pajama top.

Frank moved a straight-back chair next to the bed, and sat down. He looked at Truewell briefly, cleared his throat, and then glanced down the ward to the RN. The nurse never looked up.

Satisfied, Frank leaned close, and in a whisper, said, "Mr. True-well, my name is Frank Graham. I'm a police detective in the Homicide Unit. I don't believe we ever met." He paused, looked down the ward again to the RN, then back to Truewell. "I'm taking a chance that you can somehow hear me." He paused again. This was crazy. Still, he leaned closer and spoke carefully: "I want to talk about Mike Finnean. I want you to know that Mike is a good detective, a good man. I want you to hear that. I want you to know it's true." Frank looked down at Truewell's hands; they were clenched tightly, pressed up against the blanket and mattress. "Mike doesn't have a family of his own, but his mother is still alive, and he's got a sister and a couple of nieces." Frank blinked back sudden, surprising tears. "He's in the Knights, you know, and every Thanksgiving he's out all day delivering those food baskets that they make up for the needy. All those turkeys and canned peas and cranberry sauce. I can re-member one year when—"

A screeching noise echoed down the ward, freezing Frank in mid-sentence. The RN, moving his chair on the linoleum. Frank looked around quickly, but the RN was still bent over his paper. He turned back—

Directly into the cold steady gaze of Jimmy Truewell.

Frank jerked back against the chair, blinking rapidly. "*Jesus*...!"

The old man's head had turned, ever so slightly, and his eyes had shifted from looking out the window....

To looking at him.

The body was in coma, face a drawn, leather mask, but the eyes were very much awake. Awake and aware. They stared at him, stared right into him. *I know you now*, they said; *I know you now*....

And Frank realized that by coming here he had made the single, greatest mistake of his life. The ultimate mistake. "Oh my God," he whispered. I told you my name. Oh my God. *I told you my name!*

Halfway up the stairs to the squad room two vice detectives stopped him to offer their awkward condolences. "What do you mean?" Frank demanded. There was a siren going off in his head, loud, loud. "What the hell are you guys *talking about?*"

The squad room went silent as he burst in, as everyone stopped, for the briefest instant, to glance at him. He turned to the duty sergeant. "Is it true, Joe?" He looked at Finnean's empty desk, then his name, still redded out on the board.

The duty sergeant nodded, his face wracked in tragedy. "Yes, Detective, it's—"

"I'm going home," Frank said. "I don't feel so good. Red me out for the rest of the day, will you?"

"Sure, Detective, sure—"

But Frank was already gone.

From his living room chair, Frank stared at the phone as it rang. In the last two hours, it had rung sixteen separate times. He hadn't answered it, of course. Just sat there, hollow-eyed, listening to the rings echo through the empty house.

I told him my name, he thought, over and over. *I told him my name!*

This time, his daughter burst into the kitchen on the fifth ring. "Hey!" she yelled, dropping something on the counter with a thud. "Isn't anybody home?"

Frank stumbled to his feet, "Julie! Don't answer the—!"

But she already had. "Graham residence," he heard her say, always polite, "…Yes? Sure. One second, please, I'll see."

Frank fell back in his chair, gulping air—

Julie's voice rose. "Dad? Are you home?"

He knows my name.

His heart staccato'd, knife blades, suddenly plunging—

"Dad?"

Staccato'd, *ripped—*

She poked her head around the door. "Hey, there you are. Were you asleep?"

Frank looked at the receiver in her hand as his heart tried

once, twice…

    "Here." She held the phone out. "It's for you."

Killer

There is a ditch.
In an otherwise empty field of rye.
Below a grey, cold, lowering sky.
Western Iowa. Kansas. Nebraska.
Eastern Wyoming, maybe.
Winter.
The ditch is shallow, its rich, black earth plowed up all along its length
by the huge waffle tracks of farm machinery.
A hidden scattering of geometric puddles, down there, frozen solid.
And the remains of bodies.
Fragments of a man. Pieces of a woman.
The woman's dulled, upturned eyes reflect the cold grey of the sky.
Silence, in the ditch. Silence and secrets.
Then an eyelid moves, shifts, bulges, *and a bug crawls out.*
A shiny black and orange sexton beetle.
It clings to the woman's eyebrow, antennae waving.
Then the woman's lips move, and with a tongue as grey as her eyes she
whispers—

Cal spasmed under his blanket, his eyes opening on a cold,
hard winter morning.

He sat up slowly, grunting with the effort. The air was musty
and sour in the close, cramped bedroom. He pushed the blanket

from him and kicked crumpled, empty beer cans aside to find a flat place to put his feet. With his left hand he ran his fingers through his thinning, dishwater grey hair, using his calluses and the nubs of his ravaged yellow fingernails for a comb.

His right hand, thin and white and twisted, lay limp across his thigh. "My sacrifice to the grim reaper," he had told Ernie, the bartender at the Starlight, after the hatchet men in white had finally let him out of the free clinic in Wheatland, "gave away a little piece of myself to get a few extra innings, you know?" Small price to pay, I guess, Ernie had said. "You know it, Ernie-my-man. Hell, long as I got one left to wipe my ass and lift a brew, right?"

He shrugged his shoulder, and his dead hand flopped over.

Small price indeed.

A cat rose from the windowsill, stretched stiffly, and me-owed.

Cal lurched up, out of the bedroom, shuffled down the short, dark hall to the kitchen, and got a fresh beer from the Frigidaire. He downed it in quick, convulsive swallows, swishing the last mouthful through his cheeks, in and among the canyons and buttes of what remained of his teeth. Then he spit the frothy, phlegmy mess into the sink.

He looked for blood, but this time there wasn't any.

"You ought to go see a doctor about that, Cal."

"What–?" Cal turned, his wife's voice hanging there in the air, in his *ears*, but of course the kitchen was empty. The whole house was, except for the cats. His wife wasn't there. His wife wasn't even–

There is a ditch–

He crumpled the empty can, and then tossed it to the floor to join its comrades, dead soldiers all. A black and orange beetle skittered for cover.

There were three cats, now, arching against his shins. All the inside ones. The ones the outside cats would tear up if ever they got together.

Inside cats and outside cats.

Cal felt like an inside cat, now. Except to go to the Starlight once to drink beer and jaw with Ernie, and to the Piggly Wiggly on the interstate to stock up after the pension check came, he hadn't left the house all week. Afraid of what might be out there, waiting to tear him to shreds, if he was stupid enough to let it....

There was no need to go out anyway, not any more. Not since—

The cats meowed louder, riding his sock up his knobby shin in their impatience to be fed.

"Okay," he said, belching as he stooped to scratch each of them in turn, "hold your horses, now, ladies...."

He got the cat food bag and two food bowls from the cupboard and shook a healthy amount into each. Then he doused the cat food with a little warm water and mixed it in with his fingers.

Mixed it in *good*, for the gravy.

The cats meowed together in three-part harmony. Plaintively; no nonsense, now.

"Here we go." Cal gently nudged their heads apart with one of the bowls to get it to the floor. He watched them eat for a few moments, a vague smile curving his lips. Then he returned to the bedroom and wrestled into a sweater and overalls, and a new pair of Altima hightops with Velcro straps he had found on display next to the pantyhose at the Piggly Wiggly. "Thank God for Velcro," he had told Ernie when he had shown him those sneakers. "You ever try to tie a shoe with one hand tied behind your back? Huh?" Nope, Ernie had said, can't say as I ever have. "Well it's a pistol, Ernie-my-man, a fuckin' wet pistol, let me tell you."

Outside, the winter rye drove past Cal's property in an endless succession of pale brown waves. The wind coming down from Montana never stopped, out here. He stood shivering in the blue shadows of his side yard with the other bowl of cat food cradled in the crook of his good arm. Above, the cloud cover was solid; it would probably snow before noon. Throw in the wind, it might even blizzard.

Around back he heard the heavy chain rattle and slide, but he ignored it.

There is a field.
In the center of the field is a ditch.
In the ditch is a—

The chain moved again.

Cal turned to the little porch tacked onto the side of the house where the lean-to tool shed met the chimney. He found a mouse and two voles there, laid out neatly, legs in the air, presents —offerings—from his outside cats. The voles were stiff and frozen, but the mouse was a fresh kill, and was still warm and soft. Cal put the cat food bowl down next to them, then turned to the shed, fumbled with the simple latch, and swung its crooked door wide.

"Cal! Don't you forget to feed my baby, now!"

Emily's voice, from around the front of the house.

"I do everything else around here to make ends meet! Lord knows, the least you can do is help me feed him!"

"Yes, dear," he called back, smiling stupidly, for of course Emily wasn't there. She wasn't there *at all*.

He brought out a battered metal bucket, and a sack of Purina Dog Chow. With his good hand he poured the chow halfway up to the rim of the bucket, then set it on the porch on the other side of the dead rodents.

He fumbled in his coat pocket until his hand closed over the cold brass and steel of the folded bos'n knife there.

His eyes clouded for a moment, and he frowned, clutching the knife in his pocket. Then he grabbed the pail handle, jerked around, and strode purposefully out into the field of dead grass beyond the house. At its center he came upon the ditch, and he went down heavily to his knees in the frozen black earth there, before the carcasses.

He took the bos'n knife from his pocket and pulled the blade free with his teeth.

There wasn't much meat left on them after a week, and all of it was tough, but he sawed off what he could, and ripped off the rest, throwing the pieces into the bucket.

He stood, finally, knocked the clods of dirt from his knees, wiped the knife blade on his thigh, and then snapped it shut.

Back at the house he set the bucket on the side porch, then unzipped his overalls and urinated into the bucket, taking care to soak the meat and chow thoroughly.

His piss steamed like hot lemon tea. Looked like it, too.

He considered the mouse and the voles for a moment, then scooped them up and added them to the bucket. Then he zipped back up, grabbed the bucket handle, and went around the house to the back where the remains of his garage still tilted—still defied gravity, still taunted that goddamn fuckin' wind from out of goddamn fuckin' Montana—to the place where the dog was chained.

In its two years on earth, the dog, a one hundred and twenty-five pound shit-brindle Rottweiler, had worn a near perfect circle of dirt in the grass and weeds by the garage. Right now the dog stood at the perimeter of that circle, its heavy-link forged steel chain pulled absolutely taut and level with the ground. One end of it was securely hooked to a galvanized spike corkscrewed three feet deep in the yard dirt; the other end was shackled to an equally heavy choke chain dug firmly into the dog's muscular, rock-solid neck.

The dog stood silently, impassive, staring at him with flat black eyes. The only signs it gave of being hungry were two strings of crystal drool hanging from its jowls, swinging slightly in the wind.

Cal and the dog stared at one another for almost a full minute. Every morning for a week, now, it had gone like this. Every morning he had come upon that fuckin' behemoth of a dog standing like a fuckin' bronze statue at the absolute edge of its circle of dirt, braced at the end of its fuckin' chain, waiting for him.

Seven mornings Cal had gone to the ditch in the field and brought back something for the dog to eat. Every day he had poured chow in with it; every day he had pissed in it, beer piss, acrid and clear. Or hawked in it, or shat in it. Even *puked* in it, once. Every morning for a fuckin' week, ever since he caught that bastard and Emily–

There is a field.
Wide, long, and private.
In the field is a ditch.
In the ditch is a fucking, bitching slut, and beside her a rutting, whoring, rat bastard.
Or what little is left of them.

The Rottweiler would kill him if it could, Cal knew. He had told Ernie that more than once, more than ten times, maybe more than a hundred. But Ernie had only remembered the animal when it had been a puppy shaking and piddling on his bar, all ears and paws, wet nose and pink, licking tongue. Ernie didn't know shit about it now.

Rip his throat out if it could, Cal knew. Lap up his blood, and eat his warm guts whole.

Hatred was a serious thing; in an animal, it was dead serious. Cal knew that too.

He put the bucket down in the weeds just outside the perimeter of dirt. The dog followed the bucket down, and then returned its attention to Cal.

"Come on," Cal said in a husky, broken whisper, "ask for it, you sorry sonofabitch. *Ask* for it." He nudged the bucket with the toe of his sneaker. "Come on, there ain't much left...come on, now."

Every morning; every morning for a fuckin' week.

The dog continued to stare at him with its great, black, stony eyes.

"You're gonna have to work for this today, doggo." Cal

nudged the bucket again. If the dog wanted to, it could just touch the edge of the bucket with its nose. But it didn't. It stared at him instead. At *him*.

"Come on, you sonofabitch dog; come *on!*"

In the end he kicked the bucket, kicked it with everything he had in him, kicked it so hard his dead right arm swung up and the useless meat of his hand slapped him right in the face, poked his eye, and momentarily blinded him.

"Son-of-a-BITCH!" he roared, teetering at the edge of the dirt circle, bringing his good hand up to press against the sting in his eye where the numb finger had poked it. He heard the clink of the dog's chain as a link suddenly straightened, and the perimeter—the killing perimeter, the space where the dog could *get* him—was increased a half-inch....

"Are you teasing that poor dog again, Cal? It's just going to hate you for it. Honestly, why you taunt that poor baby is beyond me! What has he ever done to deserve—Cal? Are you listening to me? Cal?"

Goddamn crazy sonofabitch dog. Every morning. Every morning for a week now.

Every. Goddamn. Morning.

The dog ate the chow and meat scattered in the dirt with methodical quickness. It smelled the mouse and voles, nudged them with its nose, and then gobbled them, too. Then it raised its massive head, regarded Cal silently for a long moment, then turned and settled itself in the dark hole where the clapboards had separated from the garage's frame.

Dismissed him.

"Cal? You leave that poor baby alone now, you hear me? You leave my baby alone!"

On the wind that drove the grey grass seas, that sang through his head like a spray of hot, fast bullets:

"Cal?"

There is a field....

The county police cruiser, a new Crown Victoria painted

dark blue and white with slick black striping, pulled into the yard some time after noon on that seventh day.

Cal heard its door slam, then the sound of boots crunching up the gravel path to his front door. He rolled off the couch, and made it to the door just as three firm knocks shook it in its frame. Cal hesitated, and then opened the door wide.

"Sheriff," he said.

The middle-aged officer, wearing black jack boots, a freshly pressed dove-grey uniform and tall, neatly blocked cream Stetson, smiled tightly. "I left my coat in the cruiser, Mr. Tubbs; you mind if I come in out of the weather?"

Cal scratched his belly, blinking. Then, "Hell no, come on in."

The sheriff shouldered past him deftly, and Cal smelled Old Spice and Neetsfort oil and the faint, pungent perfume of cordite. He closed the door, then pointed to the officer's Glock snapped snugly into its holster. "You been firing that thing today, Sheriff?"

"Yeah." The officer's eyes moved, *darted*, all about the room. "They cornered a coyote in the Reedham's barn this morning. Took four slugs before it went down. Blew its head off. *Clean* off."

Cal whistled dutifully. "That's a hundred fifty clear bounty money, ain't it?"

The sheriff nodded, his gaze ranging swiftly over the scattered beer cans, the crusted plates piled on the coffee table before the TV. And the cats, prowling silently about. "Can't award a bounty to myself though," he said. "That's the real bitch right there."

Cal shrugged. "I'd take it. I'd take it in a New York minute."

The sheriff nodded again, moving to the hall doorway, glancing on into the kitchen. Then he turned back. "I take it she's still gone?"

"Like the wind, Sheriff. Like the fuckin' Montana wind. Pardon my French." Cal moved past him to the kitchen. "Can I get you a beer?" He opened the Frigidaire and got one out for himself.

Then behind him, so close that Cal almost jumped, the sheriff said, "You living on that stuff now, Mr. Tubbs?"

Cal closed the refrigerator with his knee. "It's getting me through." He popped the can, then took a foamy slurp off the top. "Beats Emily's cooking, anyway."

"The way I hear it, Mr. Tubbs, your wife kept a pretty good table. More than one person commented on that."

Cal took another swallow of beer, his eyes bright. "No accounting for taste, I guess."

"I guess." The officer wandered back into the living room.

Cal followed him. "People been telling you things, then, Sheriff? About me and Emily? You been talking us up?"

"Just doing what comes natural, Mr. Tubbs. Me asking questions, and them answering." The sheriff, looking suddenly taller, tighter, turned and caught Cal's eye, and held fast. "A week is a long time with no word at all, don't you think?"

Cal swallowed a rising burp. "Well—"

"Nothing from your wife's sister in Cheyenne, or her aunt in…where's that aunt, Mr. Tubbs?"

"Cedar City." Cal's voice sounded hollow. "Utah. Nope, nothing from them at all."

The sheriff nodded slowly. "I checked, of course."

"I figured you would."

"And then there's that story Buck Reedham told me this morning, after we bagged that coyote's ass in his barn."

Cal sat down on his couch. Heavily. "Buck Reedham's no friend of mine, Sheriff."

"He mentioned that. He also mentioned a conversation you had at the Starlight down by the interstate the other day, little over a week ago. You frequent the Starlight, don't you, Mr. Tubbs? Run by a man named Ernie Choate?"

"Yeah," Cal heard himself say. Hollow. Dead. Somebody else talking. "I give Ernie some business every now and then. He takes my money; I drink his beer."

"Seems you were talking to this fella Ernie down there about what to do if you caught your wives in bed with another man? Or that's how Mr. Reedham understood it from a couple of stools down the bar. Did you really have a conversation with the bartender on that subject, Mr. Tubbs? About what to do about a cheating wife?"

Cal looked down at his beer. "You could ask Ernie."

"Oh I did. Believe me, I did." Then, softly, calmly: "Do you remember what you told the bartender, Mr. Tubbs?"

"Yeah." So hollow. So dead. "I remember."

The sheriff waited a moment, then he said, "You don't want to tell me what you said, Mr. Tubbs? You got a reason why you don't want to tell me?"

"Hell no!" Cal's eyes blazed defiantly for a moment before they dulled again. "I said…I said I'd probably shoot the bastard, then cut him up into little pieces and feed him to the hogs." He swallowed. "Hogs'd eat anything, I said. Anything at all."

The sheriff lowered himself to one knee; Cal heard the creak in the leather of his holster, in his shiny black jack boots. "You wouldn't happen to keep any hogs on the property, would you, Mr. Tubbs?"

Cal took in a slow, ragged breath, hearing the rattle of the dog's chain in his head, then looked up blearily. "Sounds like you think something *happened*, Sheriff."

"*Happened*." The officer rose. "Oh, yeah. Something *happened*, all right." He placed his hands on his hips. "After a week some people start thinking about a number of things that might have *happened*, Mr. Tubbs." He shifted his gaze to the side window. "After a week maybe I've got to start looking at things a little bit *differently*, if you know what I mean."

Quietly, almost whispering, Cal said, "I don't think you better ask me any more questions, Sheriff."

"You want me to leave, Mr. Tubbs?" The sheriff smiled slightly, revealing a thin slice of white teeth. "You ordering me out of your home?"

Cal stood shakily. "Yeah," he said, "real politely, but yeah. I got that right, haven't I?"

The sheriff nodded, his smile frozen. Then he turned to the

front door, paused, and turned around. "Folks say you've been keeping to yourself this past week. Haven't left the place even once, they say."

"That don't mean nothing," Cal said. "That don't mean nothing at all."

"The bartender at the Starlight says you never miss your Friday night beer. Not for the past couple of years, anyway."

Cal couldn't keep his voice from shaking as he said, "I just *told* you to please *leave—*"

"Unfortunately, Mr. Tubbs, I got some bad news this morning." The sheriff leaned on the door. "Up until this morning, I only had one reported missing person in this entire county." He held up a long, pale finger. "Just one."

"Emily," Cal said, stone-faced. "I *know* that."

The sheriff raised a second finger. "Feed salesman named Loman, out of Wheatland. His wife said he hadn't called in a few days, and the company he shills for says he hasn't been around either."

Over his shoulder, through the door glass, Cal saw the rye grass in the field, beckoning. Slowly, carefully, he said, "You saying this guy and my wife...maybe run off together?"

The sheriff shook his head. "That would be too easy, Mr. Tubbs, too pat, don't you think?"

"This farm was my wife's life, Sheriff. This house, the animals...me."

The sheriff nodded again, with just a sliver of a smile. "Nothing but corn cobs to chew on, then, I guess, eh?"

"Corn cobs? What the hell are you talking about?"

"The hogs, Mr. Tubbs." The sheriff opened the door on a stiff, biting wind. "Hogs'll eat anything...isn't that what you said?"

There is a field.
There
Is
A

FIELD.

The blizzard hit with full, howling force by one o'clock, but that was all right. That was just fine. A good, thick blanket of snow to cover things, to *keep* things for a little while longer....

He went out into the middle of it with his dad's old nickel-plated .45 and killed the dog where it lay in the shelter of the leaning garage. It took four bullets, just like the coyote...just like Emily...but he shot the bastard's head off.

Clean off.

"I brought it home for you, Emily," he said hoarsely, struggling with the words. "I brought that damn dog home for you, you bitch. For YOU!"

Then he shoved the burning metal of the automatic's muzzle into his mouth, closed his eyes on the sudden pain, on the tears that rolled coldly through the ruined stubble of his cheeks—

"Cal! You come in the house, now. It's snowing, for goodness sake! Cal!"

He let the muzzle fall from his lips.

"Cal!"

"Yes, dear." His words were lost in the falling snow. For a moment, he wasn't even certain he had said them aloud.

"Cal?"

"Coming."

He turned, cradling the gun in the crook of his good arm, and went back to the house, the empty house, the house still full of *her*, and waited for the sheriff to return.

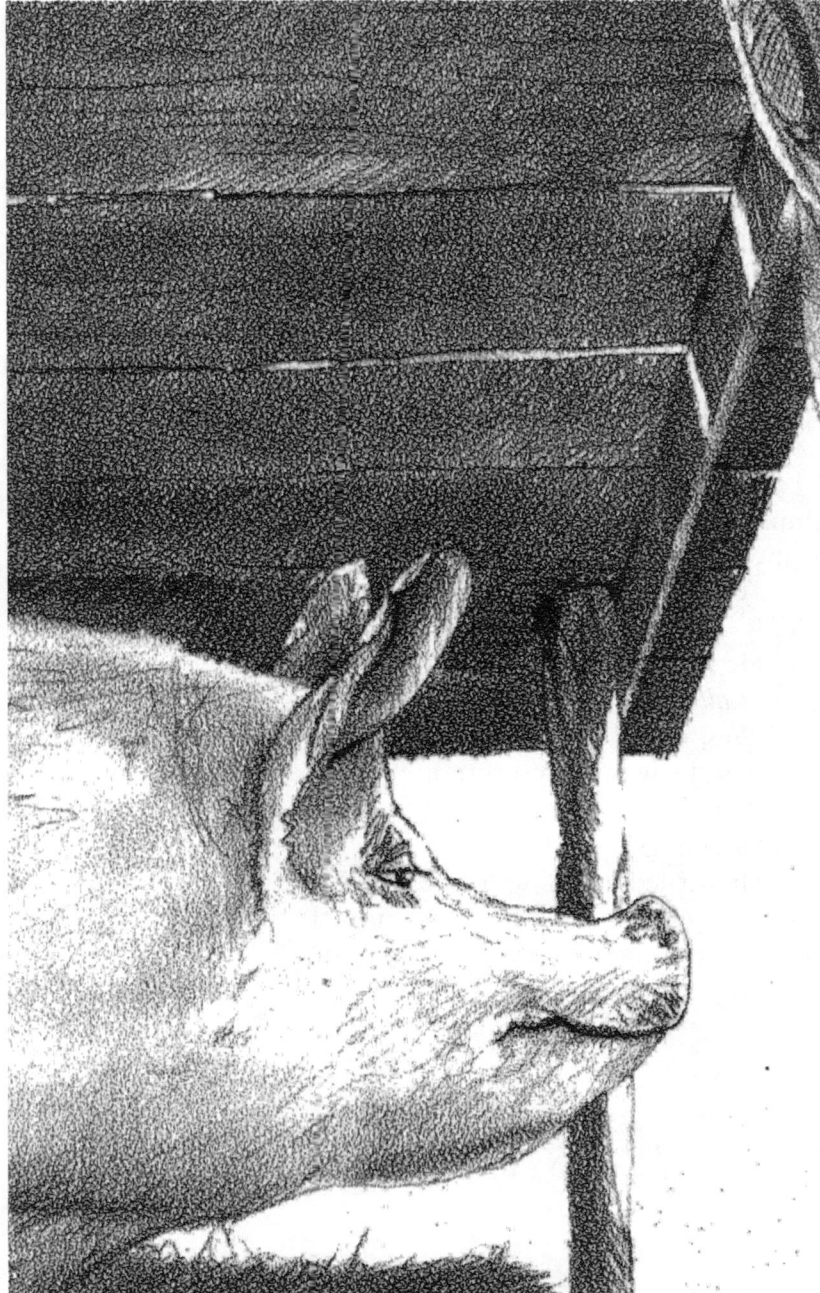

La Hermanita

Sometime after dawn, Augustin hoisted little Juanita high on his back, her arms clasped tightly around his neck, her cheek resting on the back of his head. "There," the boy said, looking down the road. "Are you more comfortable, little sister?"

"Yes, it's better."

"Good. Soon we'll reach the next town. Then we will get money for the doctor." Yes, he thought bitterly, we will beg, we will grub for the pesetas, for the thin shiny coins thrown by the rich American tourists. We will be beggars for them.

"How is your leg, Juanita?"

"The same, brother. It still hurts. Will the doctor fix it?"

"Don't worry about that. I will find you the best doctor, even if we have to walk all the way to Taxco. Please don't worry."

The cold was driven back to the shadows as the morning unfolded, and the boy soon had to pull his cap low over his eyes to avoid the warming glare.

"Are you all right, little sister?"

"Yes, Augustin."

They walked on in silence.

Towards midday, just outside a mud-baked sleepy town, brother and sister overtook a farmer leading his mule and cart. The mule sniffed, wrinkling its nostrils. Then it snorted, tossed its head and almost broke rein, but the farmer had a steady hand

and a secure grip. He hurried the animal forward, grimacing at the two, cursing them. Then he and his mule were gone, around a bend in the road, into the town.

The dust drifted.

"People don't like us," Augustin said quietly.

"But we didn't do anything."

"We never do."

The town.

Augustin walked slowly down the main street of dried mud, holding little Juanita tight against his back. There were only a few shops and buildings, a raised, boarded sidewalk, pigs, a few goats, and chickens. The pigs grunted suspiciously in the shade under the sidewalk. The chickens flew squawking in cumbersome leaps before the two, scattering feathers. The boy caught one of the feathers with his free hand and gave it to his sister; it fluttered from her fingers to the ground.

A few men came out of a shop to see what had stirred the animals.

"Vayan!" One of them said gruffly, recognizing Augustin and Juanita. "Vayan! Vayan!" and Augustin remembered with a sinking groan that he and his sister had passed through this town before. It would be no good. There would be no money here, no one to help, to take pity on them.

"Vayan!" Yelled the dark, unshaven men together. Go! Go!

Augustin turned around. "We made a mistake," he whispered to Juanita. "We must leave, try the next town. No one will help us here."

"But I hurt, Augustin. I hurt badly."

Augustin set his lips in a thin line, and turned back to the men. "One peseta!" He yelled at them. "Just one peseta!"

"You are mad, boy," one of the men said loudly. "Don't spread your madness among us. Go away before I get my gun." The other two proceeded to sit down in creaking wicker chairs in front of the shop, their faces glistening, armpits black with sweat. The one still standing spat into the street, and put his hands on his hips.

Augustin hung his head, and began walking down the street. Juanita was silent.

Suddenly there was a rumble, a squeal of metal on metal, a scattering and crunching of gravel. A car. It came into the little town very fast, slowing only at the last moment in front of the shops.

The chickens renewed their cackling, the pigs their grunting. One of the goats scampered away. The men on the raised sidewalk did not move. The car meant only one thing to them: turistas blancos. Americanos cerdos.

The car dazzled Augustin. He had not seen many in his short lifetime, certainly none this beautiful. It was pearly white, with shining chrome and sparkling windows, rich black tires with silver platter hubcaps. It rumbled like some great beast. He was a little bit afraid, standing so close to it.

A man in a suit emerged from the side of the car facing the shops, blinking in the sun, wiping his forehead with a white handkerchief. He waved to the men on the sidewalk. "Gas," he said in a loud voice. "Gasolina para mi automovil" in a forced, stumbling accent.

The man who was still standing, the one who had threatened Augustin and his sister about his gun, turned to one of the sitting men and said, "Get the Father. He speaks English."

The other nodded as he stood, and jumped down to the street. "In a moment," he said to the tourist.

"En un…" The tourist's face lapsed into confusion, then cleared. "Oh yes, I mean sí. En un momento. Bueno."

The two stood silently for a long moment, then the tourist, realizing, dug into his pocket and brought out a new peso. He tossed it to the man, who caught it, smiled, and began walking down the street to the church.

The tourist looked around.

Augustin's eyes had lighted at the sight of the coin. An entire peso! He tried to catch the tourist's attention. The man saw him, did a double take, then retreated quickly into his car.

"People do not like us," Juanita whispered into Augustin's ear.

The man standing on the sidewalk still looked in Augustin's direction, frowning, but the boy walked determinedly over to the car. There was a woman on the passenger side, wearing a fur.

He tapped politely on the glass. The window whispered down an inch, and a large coin fell out, ringing off the side of the car, falling to the ground. Augustin stooped to get it, and before the window went back up he heard a stifled scream.

It was a ten peso piece. Augustin held it in the palm of his hand, not believing what he saw. Ten pesos! He was beside himself in amazement and joy. He showed it to his sister, then thrust it deep into his trouser pocket. Then he skipped down the dusty street, stopped, showered many thank-you's on the car and the tourists inside, then continued down the street, out of the town.

Standing in the door of the church, the priest had witnessed the entire scene. He shook his head, his expression dark, and walked briskly down the street to the car.

The driver's side window came down, and cold air billowed out.

"You should not have done that," the priest said. "Now we will never get rid of him."

"What?" The tourist was open-mouthed. "You mean the money? We had to get him away from the car. God, what was that he had on his back?"

The priest sighed. "A little girl, the sister of the boy. They are orphans. He has been carrying her around like that for a month now, ever since the accident that killed their parents and injured her leg."

"But she's, I mean, surely she's..."

"Yes. She is dead."

"Oh my God," the wife said, over and over.

"Her leg became infected and she could not walk. The brother had to carry her constantly. She died while still on his back, and he would not take her off. He still carries her wherever he goes, and talks to her. He is quite mad."

"But can't someone get her off? Force him? He's just a boy."

"This was tried, one night when the boy slept, but the arms of the girl were set rigidly, too close about his neck, and the smell...but we must not talk of this." The priest smiled. "You say you need gasoline?"

Augustin walked steadily, whistling a happy tune. "With ten pesos we can cure you, little sister."

"Soon, Augustin? Soon?"

"Yes, very soon. We will find a doctor in Taxco."

"I hurt, Augustin. I hurt badly."

"Shh. I know. Don't worry."

"I—"

"Shh."

In the Stacks

There were two hundred and thirty-seven concrete sidewalk squares from the top step of the Poplar Avenue subway to the bottom step of the Chestnut Street Library. David counted them every day, twice, going to work and going home. Twenty-three of the concrete squares had a crack, edge to edge. Seventeen squares had two such cracks, and ten of the squares had three.

Today, Wednesday, the twenty-seventh day of the month, David stopped before a sidewalk square that only yesterday had had two cracks. Today there was a third crack, brand new, a small one at the northwest corner, connecting the west edge with the north edge. Today, therefore, there were now *sixteen* sidewalk squares with two cracks, and *eleven* squares with three. No problemo, David thought. Things changed; he knew that.

He continued on his way.

The Chestnut Street Library had fifteen stone steps leading up to two heavy bronze doors. The employee entrance in the alley had one step and one door. The library opened for business at nine o'clock. Mrs. Cooper, the head librarian, expected her employees to arrive at least fifteen minutes before the doors officially opened, but because of the subway schedule, David could never arrive before 8:50. Today, perhaps because he had stopped to look at the fourteenth sidewalk square out of

seventeen with *two* cracks that was now the ninth square out of
eleven with *three*, the time-clock printed "8:58" on his card when
he punched in.

"Cutting it close today, Davie," said Mrs. Cooper, peering
over her tortoise-shell glasses, stirring her cup of coffee. "You're
officially late after nine, you know. That's the rule."

David almost said, "There was a new crack," but he knew
to keep that to himself. "And please don't call me Davie. My
name is David." He wanted to say that, too. He did not like
being called "Davie" because it made him sound like a child. He
was nineteen years, three months, and four days old today, and
that was certainly not the age of a child. So he punished Mrs.
Cooper by answering with just two words: "I'm sorry," he said.

"Can't abide lateness, now," Mrs. Cooper said. "Not even
from the likes of you, Davie-My-Boy."

"No problemo," David almost said, but instead he replaced
his time card in the slot with his name: DAVID BROWN printed
over it, and went to the coat rack to hang up his jacket. No
problemo, Pedro.

Library patrons were never allowed in the stacks. It was
another library rule. Patrons had a procedure to follow when
they wanted a book. When they found what they wanted in the
card catalog or on one of the computer terminals, they wrote the
name of the book on a book retrieval card. There were spaces
for up to eight books on a card. There were also spaces for the
patrons to put their own name, and their seat number. Every seat
had a number on a small metal plate nailed to the backrest.

Completed book retrieval cards were put in an open wood
box near the doorway to the stacks. Book runners took the cards,
found the books in the stacks, and delivered them to the proper
patrons according to their seat numbers.

David was a book runner, and he was a good one. There
were ten thousand six hundred and eighty-three books available
for viewing and lending in the stacks of the Chestnut Street
Library, and David knew the location of every single one of

them. If a book was on a shelf in the stacks, then it was in his
head, too, as clear as his name, his age, how many sidewalk
squares had two cracks, and how many had three. This was why
he was good at his job. This was why he made enough money to
pay his room rent, and have dinner at the Pine Street Diner
every night, and see a movie at the Rialto every Saturday
afternoon. This week the Wednesday diner special was meatloaf. And this week, also on Wednesday, the movie changed. A
Buddy Comedy Caper with Strong Language and Sexual Situ-
ations was leaving, and a Military Thriller with Strong Language, Violence and Brief Nudity was taking its place.

"You're late," Maggie said, passing him.

David turned. Maggie was a book runner too. She waved a
small stack of book retrieval cards over her shoulder. "Don't
sweat it, Dave," she said, "I've got the first batch."

Dave was an okay name. David didn't mind it. Coming
from Maggie, it sounded almost as grown-up as "David." He
liked Maggie, and he knew she liked him, too.

Outside, in the Reading Room, he found only one book
retrieval card in the open box. He took it out and read it
carefully. There was one book requested: *The Mound Builders of
Ancient America* by Robert Silverberg. David blinked. New York
Graphic Society Limited, Copyright 1968, Library of Congress
Catalogue Card Number 68-12370. In the Chestnut Street
Library, the Card Catalogue Number was 68-1788. Aisle 12,
Row Three, Shelf Two, thirteenth slot from the left. David
looked out across the sea of reading tables and the scattering of
patrons. The seat number on the card was 57, and an elderly
man wearing a fedora-style grey hat was sitting in Seat 57,
looking right at him. He was tapping his fingers on an open page
of a spiral-bound notebook. He looked like he was In A Hurry.
Most patrons were In A Hurry. David turned, card in hand, and
went into the stacks.

He heard Maggie several aisles over, whistling quietly as she
pulled books. Whistling was not allowed in the library, not even
in the stacks, but Maggie did it anyway. She was a college

student, drove a little green car, and her dark brown hair had too many curls for David to count accurately. And she wasn't afraid of Mrs. Cooper.

The aisle, stack and shelf location of *The Mound Builders of Ancient America* by Robert Silverberg remained clear in David's mind as he went deeper into the stacks, verifying what he already knew, down the last aisle, up the stack, along the shelf, reaching with his left hand....

But it was not there.

David stared.

The Mound Builders of Ancient America was not in the thirteenth slot. In its place was a book David had never seen before. It was thick, tall, with a pale blue cloth binding. The printing on the spine was faded, hinting of gold leaf. David bent close to read the title, but the alphabet was unfamiliar, the words indecipherable. Someone must have put a book from the foreign language section here by mistake.

He pulled the book off the shelf and opened it. It smelled musty and old. He turned the pages to the light. The same strange alphabet filled them. He couldn't read any of it. He turned to the rear endleaf to read the envelope and return card. Those would be in English. But the endleaf was blank. There was no envelope, and no return card. He snapped the book shut, startling at the sound, and put it back on the shelf so quickly he nearly knocked one of the books next to it back into the adjoining shelf.

He heard Maggie in the next aisle. "Maggie!" he nearly yelled, and the tremor in his voice was clear. She came around to his aisle with wide eyes and a finger over her lips. Then she saw his expression. "What's up, Dave? What's wrong?"

He showed her the book retrieval card. "It's not there," he said. His voice still trembled. "There's another book there instead."

She frowned, reached past him, pulled a book, and handed it to him. "You mean this one?"

David looked down at it. It was *The Mound Builders of Ancient*

America by Robert Silverberg, New York Graphic Society Limited, copyright 1968. He looked down to the shelf. There was only one empty slot, the thirteenth slot. The blue book printed in the strange alphabet was gone.

"Hey, Dave," Maggie nearly touched his shoulder, "Are you okay?"

David nodded jerkily. He put the book under his arm. "Yes," he said. "I'm fine."

She kept her hand near him. "You sure?"

He jerked his head again. "No problemo."

"Okay, then, Pedro." She flashed him a quick grin. "Now go deliver your book."

Outside, in the Reading Room, David made a beeline to Seat Number 57. The elderly man had taken off his hat, but he was still drumming his fingers impatiently. "About *time*," he whispered, taking the book from David.

David wanted to tell him he was late because of the strange blue book that had appeared and then disappeared, and how the book he wanted had disappeared and then reappeared, but he knew better than to say that. He bowed his head instead, saying nothing, and returned to the wooden box. There were three new book retrieval cards in it. He took a deep breath, scooped them up, and went back into the stacks.

Outside the brownstone where he lived, someone had drawn graffiti in blue chalk on the three squares of sidewalk touching the bottom step of the stoop. David saw suns and sunbeams, flocks of birds in the shape of lower-case "M"s, lollypop trees with holes in the trunks, big, puffy clouds, and a rainbow. All of it in blue chalk. He stood at the edge of the vast drawing, and knew he couldn't walk on it. If he walked on it, he might fall *into* it.

"Whatta you waiting for, kid, the bus?"

David looked up.

Mr. Hartz, the old man who lived in the first-floor front apartment, leered at him from his open window. David had learned that talking to Mr. Hartz never worked. Talking to him made it worse. Smiling sometimes helped, so standing safely on the sidewalk square next to the first one covered in blue chalk, David smiled. Mr. Hartz took a swig from his beer can. "You're nuts, you know that, kid? Nuttier than a friggin' Mars Bar. You know that?"

David knew a lot of things. He knew that strange blue books in foreign languages didn't suddenly appear and disappear, and that books like *The Mound Builders of Ancient America* by Robert Silverberg didn't disappear and then suddenly reappear, either. He also knew that when he was small, when he had been a very little boy, any change like this would have made him curl up in a ball in the corner and just scream.... But he was nineteen years, three months and four days old today; he wasn't a little boy; he was a grown-up. His name was David, not Davie. He would not curl up; he would not scream.

But he was certain that if he walked on the sidewalk squares that touched his bottom stoop step, he would fall through them into a vast, empty blue sky. He would fall through that sky, and fall, and fall....

He wondered: what would Dr. Mooney say if he told her that?

"Hey buddy! D'you *mind?*"

A man in a rumpled gray suit, with a Styrofoam cup of coffee in one hand and a black imitation leather briefcase in the other, sidled past him, shooting a disgruntled look over his shoulder as he walked over the chalk drawing.

"Fruitcake," Mr. Hartz said from his window. "Mars bar."

David turned away, took in a deep breath, and walked back down the block. He could have his meatloaf at the Pine Street Diner in his work clothes. He could eat his peas without having washed his face, without having collected and opened his mail, without having opened the window to the airshaft to let out the hot, close air that had accumulated in his little apartment during the day. He could do and *not do* all of these things. He could do something *new*. It would be all right. It would be no problemo.

In the Pine Street Diner, the waitress behind the counter brought David his meatloaf, mashed potatoes and green peas without him having to ask. "I came straight here tonight," he told her as she put a glass of milk down for him. "From work."

"Did you now," she said.

Later, with the evening shadows long and cool along the street where he lived, he found that someone had washed the sidewalk in front of the stoop. All of the chalk drawings were gone. Only a faint haze of color remained. Still, he hesitated.

From his window overlooking the street, Mr. Hartz said, "What are you waiting for, kid, an engraved invitation?"

David looked up, smiled, and went quickly across the newly washed sidewalk, up the four stoop steps, and into the building. I'm safe, he thought. "I'm safe," he said, in the dark hallway that always smelled like urine and boiled cabbage.

Mr. Hartz yelled through his door: "Mars bar!"

There were two hundred and thirty-seven concrete sidewalk squares from the top step of the Poplar Avenue subway to the bottom step of the Chestnut Street Library. This had been the case for one year, one month and thirteen days, ever since his first day of work at the library. But when he reached the Library today he stood in the center of the two hundred and thirty-seventh square...and looked down at one more sidewalk square, a new square, the two hundred and thirty-*eighth*. Its near edge touched the square he stood on, and its far edge touched the library's bottom step. Like the sidewalk squares in front of his apartment house the previous evening, it was covered in scribblings of blue chalk, a fathomless, featureless blue.

He heard a noise, a soft, mewling sound, like someone very sad, or very afraid. Then he realized *he* was making the sound. His eyes welled, and hot tears tracked down both of his cheeks. Don't fall, he told himself, blinking furiously. Don't fall into the blue square. Stand *straight*.

"Hey Dave, come on, we're going to be late."

Maggie passed him, went two steps toward the side alley, then stopped and turned back, her dark curls flying. "Dave, you coming?" Then she saw the tears, and she came back to him. She came close enough to speak very quietly, so only he could hear her. She said, "What's wrong, David? Why are you crying?"

He wiped his cheeks with the palms of his hands. "I have to see Dr. Mooney."

"Your old shrink? But I thought—" She stopped, then started again, gently, "Don't you need an appointment?"

"I have to see Dr. Mocney," he said again. He felt his nose running, so he sniffed.

"Sure," Maggie said, nodding, "you go do that. I'll cover for you here, don't worry."

"Mrs. Cooper—"

"Don't worry, I'll handle her." Maggie reached across the small empty space between them and touched his arm. It felt like a bee sting, but he didn't flinch. He knew she didn't mean it. "No problemo," she said, "okay?"

There was a bench just inside the front entrance of Dr. Mooney's office building. Two large-leafed ferns in black pots flanked it. Two elevators took up the opposite wall. On the narrow section of wall between them was a tenant directory, framed in aluminum and glass. There were one thousand nine hundred and six white plastic letters pushed into the black velvet of the directory. The building had twelve floors, and forty-seven tenants. Dr. Mooney's office was on the sixth floor. Counting down from the top, her directory listing number was twenty-two.

David sat with his knees drawn up to his chest, under the overarching fronds of the plant farthest away from the entrance doors. He fixed his gaze to the floor. He counted the feet of the people who passed him, entering and leaving the elevators. By lunchtime he had counted one hundred and twenty-six legs, sixty-three people, thirty-seven men, twenty-four women, and two children. None of them was Dr. Mooney.

Outside, through the glass doors, he heard a church bell

ring twelve times. David's stomach was empty, and he had to go to the bathroom. More feet came and went, and he counted them. Then a pair of feet he recognized stopped in front of him, and David looked up.

"David," Dr. Mooney said, leaning down toward him, "what are you doing here?"

"I have to pee," David said. Then, "Your hair is red."

She raised her hand to touch the side of her bun. "Yes it is, David. Thank you for noticing."

"Has it always been red?" His lower lip trembled, all by itself. Then he began the mewling sound again. "Last time," he said, "was your hair red?"

"Come." She reached for his arm, stopping a half-inch away. "Get up, David, will you? Come with me."

"I have to pee," he said again.

"I know you do. You can use the bathroom in my office."

He stood, and his legs tingled. "The green bathroom?"

"Yes," she said, hesitating only a moment, "the green bathroom."

There were still two thousand eight hundred and eighty-six pale green floor tiles in Dr. Mooney's office bathroom. David counted them twice, to be sure. When he finally emerged, he found Dr. Mooney seated behind her desk. She smiled at him, and indicated the stuffed leather chair by the window.

David sat, his back straight, hands folded in his lap.

"Feeling better?" Dr. Mooney asked.

David said, "There was a an extra sidewalk square."

Dr. Mooney leaned forward. "David," she said, "you remember, don't you, that I'm not your doctor any more?"

"There were always two hundred and thirty-*seven* sidewalk squares," David said. "Today there was two hundred and thirty-*eight*." He blinked away sudden tears.

"You are supposed to see Dr. Lieberman now," Dr. Mooney said, "at the Oak Street Clinic. I introduced you to him. We went there together, you and I, remember?"

"The extra sidewalk square was blue," David said. "Why

was there an extra square? Why was it blue?"

"Maybe the Public Works Department did some repair work. They fix things and paint things all the time." She put her hand on the phone. "I called Dr. Lieberman while you were in the bathroom."

"In the library," David said, "there was a book that wasn't supposed to be there."

"Libraries buy new books all the time—"

"*The Mound Builders of Ancient America* by Robert Silverberg was supposed to be there, in the thirteenth slot, but it wasn't. A blue book was there instead. It had gold letters, and a strange alphabet." Tears rolled down his cheeks unhindered. "I couldn't read it."

Dr. Mooney pushed her tissue box across the desk toward him, and then she picked up her phone.

David abruptly stood. "I have to go," he said, wiping his cheeks with his palms, then wiping his palms on his pants. "I have to go back to the library." He turned, and took three steps toward the door. "I'm supposed to be there."

Dr. Mooney rose. "Are you sure that's wise, David? Perhaps—"

"Maggie is covering for me," he said.

"David—" Dr. Mooney began, but he didn't hear what she said next, because he was already through the door and halfway across the reception room. "Mr. Brown," the receptionist said, looking up, smiling as he passed her, "So good to see you again."

He stopped, turned, said, "I have to know," and then he left.

There were fifteen stone steps that led up to two bronze doors at the Chestnut Street Library. David counted them all. Inside, past the dimly lit vestibule with its marble pedestals and dusty busts of famous Victorian poets, he went through another set of double doors and entered the Reading Room. As he pushed through the turnstile the librarian behind the checkout desk glanced up, peering briefly over her tortoise-shell glasses, then returned to her work.

David went over to the standing table near the card catalog. On the table were boxes of pencils, and stacks of book retrieval cards in cubbies. He picked the sharpest pencil he could find, and carefully printed the name of the book he wanted on one of the cards. Then he looked out into the Reading Room, saw that Seat Number 22 was empty, and wrote its number on the card. He put the card in the open box next to the doorway to the stacks, and then went to his seat to wait.

A young woman with dark curly hair came out of the doorway to the stacks a few minutes later, scooped out the book retrieval cards, and disappeared back into the stacks.

David began counting.

When he reached three hundred and thirteen, the young woman reappeared with four books under her arm. There were book retrieval cards sticking out of three of them. She took two of the books to an elderly lady sitting in Seat Number 36, and another book to a teenager in Seat Number 77. She brought the last book to David.

"I don't know," she whispered, smiling. "You must really like this book!"

He took it from her. It was blue, with faded gold lettering on its spine. When he opened it, it smelled musty and old. He looked at the open pages, blinking rapidly. The printed text was at first a jumbled sea of odd, apocryphal symbols. But then, but *then*.... He looked up in wonder. "I can read this," he said.

The young woman's smile broadened. "You know, you're starting to get me interested in archeology now." Then she saw his expression, and her smile faded. A faint frown of concern creased the space between her eyebrows. "Are you okay?"

"Yes," he said, "I'm sorry." He nodded in two quick jerks. "I'm fine. Yes."

Across the Reading Room, the librarian looked up at them, a warning finger to her lips.

The young woman leaned close. "Hey," she whispered, "no problemo," and she winked. Then she was gone, back into the stacks.

No problemo, David thought, blinking rapidly, his eyes darting. No problemo, Pe-dro. His gaze fell once more on the words, and a calm descended. He smiled as he fell into the book, into the fathomless blue of the infinite sky, and he fell for a long, long time.

The Retirement

Upon my retirement, with no family or close friends to consider, I decided to move across the country to a state and a town entirely new to me. I purchased a little brick house—a mid-century gem of a rancher, my realtor called it—on a quiet street just north of the downtown proper. "Close enough so you can walk to just about everything," she assured me. *Everything,* I remember thinking. *Really? Everything?*

True to her word, however, I quickly found walking destinations I either liked or needed: a small but well-stocked supermarket, a variety of restaurants and cafes, a hardware store, a park, a fine old library, a bakery, even a cemetery.

Charles Midwich, I said to myself, with no small note of satisfaction. *Retired. No: reborn.*

———

"Yes sir!" The bakery counterman, dusting flour off the front of his apron, grinned a warm greeting. "What can we get for you today?"

"One of those scones, please." I pointed into the case below. "What kind are they?"

"Blueberry cream on the left, and honey fig on the right."

"I'll have a honey fig, please."

"They're just out, not even five minutes. Melt in your mouth. Anything else?"

"A coffee, please. Medium size."

"We have light and dark roast brewed just now."

"Light is fine. And the scone." I leaned on the counter. "I'm new to the neighborhood, but when my real estate agent was describing the neighborhood, she mentioned a news agent stand somewhere along here. I haven't been able to find it."

The counterman poured my coffee into a tall ceramic mug. "Well, the bakery has been here since I was a kid, but I don't remember them ever selling newspapers." He plated the scone and put the coffee beside it. "Fixings are over there to your left." He tapped the register pad. "That'll be three fifty-four, please."

I handed him a five.

He paused making change. "Now you mention it, I think I remember my granddad saying there was a news agent around here somewhere, once upon a time. Long gone, of course."

"Maybe that's what she meant, then," I said.

My seat at the narrow bar along the bakery window afforded a fine view of the town cemetery across the street. I ate my scone and drank my coffee, marveling at the cemetery's Gothic stone entry arch and formidable turreted wall, and the extensive monument city beyond. The graves were tucked under old oaks, pines and buttonwoods in a gently rolling, well-tended landscape. That would be a good place to land the plane, I decided; that would be a good place to end up, when the time came. An unobtrusive plot in the shade of a buttonwood tree, perhaps. Or under some kind of pine that stayed green the year round.

The counterman came around with a pot of coffee. "Can I top you off? You ordered light roast, right?"

I hesitated.

"Refills are on the house."

I pushed my mug toward him. "I was admiring that fine old cemetery over there."

He poured. "Pre-Civil War, like the rest of the town."

"It must be all filled up by now, I guess."

"The cemetery?" He looked across the street. "I don't think so. I mean, I see funerals every now and then, Saturdays."

"Really. Interesting. Thanks." I raised my mug. "And thanks."

The cemetery office was attached to the turreted outer wall, just beside the entrance arch. It had rubble-stone walls, mullioned windows, and a planked door painted glossy red. I raised and lowered the heavy knocker twice before entering. The office inside reminded me of someone's cozy, well-loved study: a cluster of comfortable stuffed leather chairs around a wide stone fireplace at one end, and bookcase walls at the other, surrounding a bulky oak desk. A rather large, fleshy woman in a mint-green pants-suit sat behind the desk, and an expansive map of the cemetery grounds hung on the wall behind her. She rose, and extended a puffy pink hand. "Good morning! I'm Dotty Stroud."

Her handshake was faintly moist. I took a seat in one of the two chairs she offered. "I'm pleased to meet you," I said. "My name is Charles Midwich. I'm here about a plot."

"Of course, of course!" Dotty reseated herself with an audible exhalation, and a serene smile.

"So you're not full, then?"

"Oh no! Some sections have been closed for decades, of course." She turned to point to the map behind her. "Sections A through D, and all of E along the Memories Walk." She turned back with a look of mild concern. "I hope you don't have your heart set on one of those."

"I just want somewhere near a tree, or under one, ideally."

"I'm sure we have several like that available in Section F. Would you like to go see?"

"You mean, right now?"

"No time like the present!" She pulled a large ledger book from a desk drawer, and then a small, personal notebook from another. In moments, consulting the ledger, she compiled a short list. "You are going to love these, I believe," She closed the notebook with a snap. "You can follow me in your car if you like."

"I walked here, actually."

"Well then you can ride with me!" She reached for her handbag. "Shall we?"

Dotty's car was large and old, and smelled of violets and stale cigarette smoke. I felt around for my seat belt, but couldn't find it. The drive took us through Sections A, B and C, with impressive stone architecture and a wide variety of carved monuments and headstones, all of them moss-splotched, their edges and details softened by time. "This reminds me of something," I said, as we drove slowly under a gently curved stone pedestrian bridge.

"Have you ever visited Central Park in New York City?"

I nodded.

"Frederick Law Olmsted." Dotty's smile was just south of smug. "He designed our sanctuary first, of course."

"Wow," I said. "I'm impressed."

We passed a small curbside sign with the letter "F" on it, and I noticed a distinct change in both the trees and the monuments. Dotty noticed I noticed. "New laws and regulations," she ex-plained. "We were forced to comply, of course."

Firs and pines replaced the oaks and buttonwoods, and the elaborately carved monuments made way for more sensible rectangular stones and the occasional stylized cross. "I'm more interested in a stone like these, anyway," I said. "Something simple."

"I have a monument man you should meet with. His shop is out of town, but he'll come right to your house. He can fabricate anything you have in mind." Dotty glanced over to me. "Very sensibly priced, I might add."

As we approached a stand of pine trees a strange feeling suddenly overcame me, one that said: "Here. Right here."

"Wait." I put my hand on the metal dashboard. "Stop!"

Dotty applied her brakes. "Here?"

"Right here." I pointed across her, to an empty plot between two grey granite gravestones. "That one. Is it available?"

"It's not on my list, but we can certainly find out." She turned her car off and cracked her door. "No tree."

"I don't mind."

That strange feeling grew as I walked around the car and onto the grass. Not anxiety, not fear, quite the opposite, in fact. It felt like...excitement, like coming home. Like I belonged. Like I belonged *here*.

"Sometimes families will reserve adjacent plots," Dotty said, taking out her little notebook to jot down the names on the stones on either side, and the aisle number from the metal tag on the little stake along the curb. DEAN and CARDINUTO. She pointed to the former. "The husband is already interred, as you can see. We're just waiting for the wife."

I looked at her in alarm. "You mean she might have the empty plot reserved?"

"Oh no." She pointed to the stone again. "See the space left for the inscription? No, she'll go on top of her husband. We allow interments up to three deep, actually."

I knelt in the warm grass in the middle of the empty plot, and faced east across a gentle slope of simple stones. The trees beyond framed waves of older ones. "I like this. I really do. I hope it's available."

"I'm sure it is." Dotty consulted her list. "We still have those others to see, of course. Near the trees you wanted."

"No." I got back up, dusting my knees. "This is the one I want."

"You're sure?"

"Absolutely."

"Very well, then." She deposited her notebook in her handbag. "Let's go back to the office."

I didn't want to leave. What an odd feeling! Like leaving home. I looked around. DEAN, CARDINUTO. Behind: GREELY, ANDERSEN, RYDER, THARP...

New neighbors.

Friendly, I hoped.

Mr. Wheeler, the man from the monument company, smelling like cigars and honest sweat, took the dining room chair I offered. He handed me his business card, and then, from his black leather briefcase he produced a selection of playing-card-sized stones, and laid them in a neat row before me. "The darkest granite we offer is called Chinese Black." He pushed that sample forward. "It's from a quarry in New Hampshire, actually. It's also one of the more expensive granites we offer."

I picked it up. "I like it."

"For the size you want, we're talking close to a thousand dollars, installed."

"Not a problem." I put the sample down. "Let's go with it."

"That was easy." He pulled a form from his briefcase, and a fountain pen from his inside jacket pocket. "I'll just need your particulars. Full name and billing address and all that. And your date of birth, of course." He winked. "We'll leave that other date blank for now."

"No." I raised a finger, and actually wagged it at him. "I don't want any dates on the stone. No first name either. Just my last name. I want my stone to be simple, really simple. I only want my last name on it."

He looked at me over his glasses. "You're sure."

"Absolutely."

"Just…Midwich, then, no 'T.'" Mr. Wheeler still held his pen poised over the form.

"And all in capitals. With no serifs. You know what I mean? I want block lettering."

"We can give you sample typefaces to choose from." He made a note at last. "Centered, just high of the midline, of course."

"As long as it's big, with maybe just six inches or so on either side."

"That's certainly big." He made another note. "As soon as you pick your typeface, we'll give you a mock-up sketch for approval or changes. Can I get your email?"

"My what?"

"Your email address."

I looked at him. "I just have my home address." I could see I was confusing him, somehow. "Can you mail it to me?" I asked.

"Of course, but it'll take longer."

I folded my hands. "I'm in no hurry."

"Excuse me, sir."

I stopped and turned. A member of the cemetery grounds crew rose from beside a large monument, a pair of grass clippers in hand. He pointed with them to the small pot of daisies I held in my hands. "If you don't mind my asking, where are you going with those?"

"To my grave. My plot, I mean, the one I bought so it would be, you know, ready." I pointed in the direction of Section F. "They just installed the stone the other day."

The groundsman shook his head with an apologetic expression. "We have a strict policy, sir, no plantings by the stones."

"But I've seen others, lots of them. Flowers, mostly." I held up the pot. "Just like these."

"Not here, sir, not in Thornrose. Not since, well, years and years."

"But—"

"It's the gas-powered riding mowers, you see. We can get close up next to the stone rows, trim the grass right and proper with just a pass. Then we make it tidy with the clippers, if we need to." He pushed his fedora back. "That plant of yours would get shorn right off by the mower, you see. Shorn right off, more's the pity."

Surely there were flowers; I'd seen them. I know I had. Still, I could tell this was an argument I clearly wasn't going to win.

"Your daisies look right and healthy," the groundsman continued. "Maybe there's a spot for it in your garden at home?"

My garden? At home? "Maybe," I said.

The summer heat had come and gone, and the occasional chill October breeze felt good against my face as I sat on my plot, my back resting against my stone, reading. Reading for pleasure was something I had always promised myself, but never seemed to have the time for during my working years. I had compiled a long list of books I wanted to read once I retired, however. During my first visit to the town library I had checked, wandering among the stacks, and found it had nearly all of them!

"We just need some sort of proof of residence," the librarian had told me, "like a driver's license, for instance. Or a utility bill."

I had reached into my jacket pocket. "I have a statement from the gas company."

"Perfect!"

Now, with my new library card in my wallet, and a library book in my lap, I could read as long as there was light.

"We close at sunset, sir," a groundsman reminded me, trailing pipe smoke as he walked by with his rake.

I raised my book in acknowledgment. I could see at least three other people, sitting by their stones, reading, just like me. I knew the rules by heart; we all did.

As I watched the last autumn leaves swirl across the bakery parking lot, the counterwoman brought over my check. I looked at it and frowned. "I think you made a mistake here," I said.

"Really?" She took it from me. "One honey fig scone at thirty-five cents, and one coffee at two bits." She left a thumbprint of flour on the check when she handed it back. "Sixty cents total."

"Are you having some sort of a sale?"

She laughed. "No sir!"

"I just don't know how you're making any profit here." I reached into my pocket. "My lucky day, I guess." I handed her a dollar. "Keep the change."

"Gee, thanks!" she said.

"Are you dead?"

I opened my eyes, shading them against the afternoon glare. The silhouette of a small boy blocked the sun. "No," I said, sitting up, using my stone for support. "I was just napping."

The boy, in corduroys, buster browns, and a sweater with a cartoon rocket ship on it, frowned seriously. "I don't have to take naps any more." He couldn't have been more than four.

"Good for you," I said.

"I'm a big boy now."

"So you are. Naps are for babies anyway. And old people like me."

"I can read too." The boy pointed to my book, still tented open in my lap. "A little bit, anyway."

"Good for you," I repeated. "Reading is one of the greatest pleasures in life."

"Jeffrey!"

The boy looked over his shoulder. "That's my mom."

"Jeffrey!"

"Coming!" The boy sighed. "I got to go. Nice meeting you, mister."

"And you as well." I nodded toward his parents several plots down. "Now you'd best...."

"Yeah." He turned and skipped back to where his mother stood, and his father knelt, before a nondescript granite stone. Well beyond them, a cemetery groundsman perched on his loud, rattling driving mower, approaching slowly, probably his last cut of the season.

"What were you doing over there?" the boy's mother asked the boy, just over the rising clatter.

"Talking," he said.

"Talking?"

"To the man."

Jeffrey's mother looked in my direction. "What man?"

She and Jeffrey stood still, and Jeffrey's father continued

kneeling, as the groundsman on his mower, very slowly and carefully, so as not to mark or scratch the stones, ran his mower over their plot—ran it right through them, as though they were nothing more than air—and came on, just as slowly, just as carefully, over my plot, over me.

The Blue Cat

Miss Foyle was too old to drive, and though she disliked taking the bus, she tolerated it once a month to visit the Care and Share shop downtown to look for new Dresden porcelains to add to her collection. She had found her Woodsman and her Milkmaid there, both near pristine, and priced very reasonably. The volunteer behind the dinnerware, crockery and figurine counter clucked like a mother hen when she saw her. "Sorry, dear, no new Dresdens have come in."

"Just as well," Miss Foyle said. "I'm running out of mantel space anyway." They both shared a quiet smile.

Then Miss Foyle saw the cat.

It was a glass figurine, severely Deco, lacquered a pale powder blue everywhere except its face, chest, and paws, which were clear. Whiskers were hurried slashes of black enamel, and its eyes were awkward dabs of dark red. It sat on its haunches, front legs at full extension, tail curled around to cover one paw. Like a little Egyptian god, Miss Foyle thought, instantly taken by the piece. She pointed to it. "Can I see that please?"

"The cat?" The volunteer's eyebrows rose slightly, but she took it down from the shelf and gave it to her. It was heavy solid glass through and through, with no chips or scratches. Miss Foyle turned it over to look for a mark or price sticker, but the bottom was blank. "How much is it?" she asked.

The volunteer made a face. "It just came in, estate sale, I think. Tillie does the pricing, but she's not due in today." She shrugged. "A dollar?"

Miss Foyle did not hesitate. "Deal," she said.

She didn't notice the tiny parallel cuts on her forefinger, or the accompanying small smear of blood, until she was home and the blue cat was in its place on the mantel. "That's odd," she said aloud, and put the finger in her mouth. *How did that happen?*

"Trouble!" Miss Foyle put her cat's dish down by his water bowl, then turned again to the hallway. "Trouble! Dinnertime!" Trouble never missed a meal, except when he was in the woods behind the house, hunting. She knew he was inside because she distinctly remembered letting him in before taking her afternoon nap.

Instead of the gentle tinkling of his collar bell, however, she heard another sound, equally gentle, but…different.

Tink! Ting!

Like one of her porcelains being lightly tapped by something hard and sharp.

Tink! Ting!

Was he up on the mantel again, living up to his name, traipsing through her porcelains? "Trouble!" Miss Foyle rushed down the hallway to the parlor, then exhaled in relief. The only cat on the mantel was the glass figurine she had purchased that morning. It looked across the room at her with its dark, ruby-red eyes. Then Miss Foyle saw Trouble. He was lying on the hearthstone, directly under the mantel.

"Trouble?"

The cat didn't stir. Miss Foyle went over to him, knelt, and stroked his fur. "Trouble?" Her hand came away wet. A warm, thick wetness. She saw fresh blood on her fingers, but it took a few seconds for that to register, then a few more for her to cry out and leap back, stumbling up against the settee.

Above her, the blue cat grinned.

Tink! Ting!

The first two days following Trouble's death Miss Foyle only entered the parlor to air it out, opening the front window in the morning, and closing it before going to bed. Today, standing in the hallway before the parlor door, the air in the room still smelled faintly...foul. Like dead things. Like death itself. Her neighbor was due soon for their weekly tea and game of Hearts. She should open the window again. She should—

The doorbell chimed. Miss Foyle turned, fingers to her lips, and saw a familiar shadow against the front door curtains. Goodness, she thought, was it that time already?

Mrs. Grimsby, her neighbor two doors down, bustled past Miss Foyle before she even had the door fully open. "I'm so sorry to hear the bad news, Anne! So very sorry you lost poor Trouble!" Mrs. Grimsby made a right turn into the parlor, went over to the settee, and sat down.

Miss Foyle hesitated at the doorway.

"Well what are you doing standing there!" Mrs. Grimsby opened the side table drawer and took out the deck of cards. "Is something wrong, dear?"

Miss Foyle gave her neighbor a pained expression. "No, nothing. You're right." She entered the parlor, carefully ignoring the mantel. Mrs. Grimsby put the card deck aside and patted the cushion beside her. "Come. Sit down for heaven's sake. We'll talk about it."

Miss Foyle took the seat offered, clutching her hands together on her lap. "I should make the tea," she fretted.

"Oh forget the tea! We can have that any time." Mrs. Grimsby covered Miss Foyle's hands with one of her own, and squeezed briefly. Then she gave a brief gasp of quiet astonishment. "And who is this?"

A large cat, grey with white markings, had appeared in the parlor doorway.

"That's Jax." Miss Foyle attempted a smile. "I just got him from the shelter this morning."

"Jax!" Mrs. Grimsby bent and offered a hand. "Pleased to

meet you!"

The cat stared at the hand, then her, if briefly, then left the doorway, back the way he had come. Mrs. Grimsby chuckled. "Friendly little beast! I am glad you got another one, dear. Back on the horse, as they say."

"I know, but…" Miss Foyle blinked away new tears. "Just look at me," she said, smiling helplessly.

Mrs. Grimsby pulled a handkerchief from her sleeve and offered it, but Miss Foyle shook her head, pulled her own from the sleeve of her housedress, and dabbed at her cheeks. "It's just…" she began, "…it all started…" She waved her handkerchief at the mantel without looking, "with that cat."

Mrs. Grimsby saw the blue cat for the first time. "Oh dear! Whatever possessed you to buy that?" She got up before Miss Foyle could stop her, went to the mantel, and took the glass figurine down. "Where on earth did you get this? At a carnival sideshow? It's positively hideous!"

"Be…be careful, Agnes," Miss Foyle stammered. "You might get cut."

"Don't be silly. Cut from what, these little cracks?"

"Cracks?" That brought Miss Foyle up short. She leaned forward. "What cracks?"

Mrs. Grimsby thrust the blue cat nearly under Miss Foyle's nose. "These, dear. At the base, and along the leg."

Miss Foyle saw a hairline pattern of cracks that she knew had not been present when she bought the figurine. They were new.

"Honestly, Anne!" Mrs. Grimsby returned the blue cat to its place on the mantel. She turned, dusting her hands ceremoniously. "What were you thinking?"

Tink! Ting!

Mrs. Grimsby paused. "What was that?" Then she looked down at her hand. "And why on earth am I bleeding?"

The shelter smelled of pet urine and flea powder. Miss Foyle glimpsed row after row of cages in the ceramic-walled room behind the counter, all of them holding cats and kittens. "I'm sorry," the woman behind the counter said, closing her ledger with a loud thump. "No more cats for you I'm afraid."

Miss Foyle gripped her handbag tightly. "But...I only want one. Just one. My first cat passed away last week, you see."

The woman tapped the ledger cover with a stubby finger. "Our records show you adopted two cats since then, Miss Foyle."

"But I...I like cats," Miss Foyle said, pleading with her eyes. "And they like...company."

The woman frowned. "I'm sorry," she repeated, "but that's just too many. Too many in such a short time." She tapped on the ledger again. "People might ask why."

Miss Foyle brought her handbag up against her chest. "But–"

"I'm sorry," the woman said a final time, "but no. We have rules."

When Miss Foyle finished her weekly shopping, she saw a sign hung on the community board just inside the exit door, crudely drawn in crayon:

!!FREE KITTENS!!
10 MOTT STREET

Pushing her loaded two-wheeled cart slowly along the sidewalk, she detoured to pass Mott Street, and found another sign, very much like the first, taped to the picket fence of Number 10. As she pushed her cart up the walk a little girl with copper-red hair and lemon-colored overalls skipped across the front porch to meet her. Miss Foyle smiled at the child. "You have kittens, dear?"

The little girl nodded vigorously, pigtails flying. "Lots! Eight! Come see!" She led Miss Foyle onto the porch to a large open cardboard box. Inside, a fat grey tabby cat curled on a fuzzy towel, surrounded by her litter: three grey tabbies, one black with a white face, two mottled white and cream, another all black, and the last all grey. Most of them were asleep, but the black one and the grey one were wide-awake, tussling and pouncing.

"Mama says they're old enough now to give away," the little girl said, looking up at Miss Foyle. "Would you like one?"

Miss Foyle looked in the box again. The two kittens were rolling around like a furry grey and black ball. "Actually…would you mind if I took two?"

The grandmother clock in the downstairs hall struck five, its muted chimes filling the otherwise quiet house. Miss Foyle awoke from her nap to find both kittens—the grey and the black—asleep on her stomach. She deposited them very carefully on the coverlet beside her, then found her glasses, ran her fingers through her hair, and eased out of bed. She listened to the ticking of the clock downstairs, the quiet rush of a car going by in the street, and the far-off muffled cries of children outside playing a street game. Olly-olly-oxen-free.

Then she heard it, and jerked her head toward the door. Dear God in heaven, she thought, so soon?

Miss Foyle went downstairs, and the kittens, half-awake, tumbling and stumbling, followed. She stopped at the parlor doorway. Across the room, sitting on the fireplace mantel with her Dresden porcelains, the blue cat stared back at her. She rubbed her forefinger against her thumb, feeling the tiny scars.

She heard the sound again: *Tink! Ting!* Glass gently touching glass.

Tink! Ting!

She brought her trembling fingers to her lips, looking at the blue cat, at its ruby-red, unblinking eyes, and at the space—at least an inch on either side—between it and the nearest porcelains on the mantel. Too soon, she thought, feeling tears begin to well, much too soon! She wiped at her eyes, and then looked down at the kittens, playing at her feet.

The next morning she returned to Mott Street. The sign

was still on the gate, and the big box was still on the porch. The little red-haired girl, however, was nowhere to be seen. Miss Foyle hesitated outside the gate, but then she saw a woman kneeling in a bed of tulips beside the house. She cleared her throat. "Excuse me?"

The woman looked up, wiped her forehead with a forearm, and got to her feet. She dropped her gardening gloves. "Can I help you?"

"I was looking for the little girl." Miss Foyle pointed to the sign. "The one giving away kittens. Your daughter?"

The woman nodded. "She's at play camp." She dusted her knees, and approached the gate. "You interested in a kitten? We have a few left."

"Oh no, I'm sorry!" Miss Foyle fumbled in her coat pocket, and brought out the grey kitten. "I took this one home yesterday…but I found I was allergic."

"Allergic?"

Miss Foyle could feel her cheeks burning. "Yes…to cats. I'm allergic to cats. I'm afraid I have to return her."

The woman reached over the gate, her expression neutral. "All right, hand her over." She took the kitten from Miss Foyle, and without another word went up on the porch and deposited it in the cardboard box.

"I'm so sorry," Miss Foyle said.

The woman turned and put her hands on her hips. "No problem. You're allergic. Have a nice day."

"Hello? Anybody home?"

Miss Foyle turned, creaking in her wicker chair.

Mrs. Grimsby peeked around the corner of the house. "There you are!" She picked her way along the overgrown path to the steps of Miss Foyle's back porch. "What on earth are you doing back here? It's a jungle!"

Their tea date. Miss Foyle glanced at her wristwatch with a sinking heart. It was past two! "Oh dear!" she exclaimed, "I'm so sorry!"

Mrs. Grimsby came up the steps. "It's just so buggy back here." She took out her handkerchief, dusted the seat of the chair beside Miss Foyle, and lowered herself into it. She reached across and fingered the sleeve of Miss Foyle's dress. "We look like twins today, Anne. I always said you look your best in mauve."

Miss Foyle made to rise. "Shall I make us that tea?"

"No." Mrs. Grimsby patted Miss Foyle's knee. "Sit. Relax. You look tired, dear. You don't look well."

"It has been…a trying week," Miss Foyle admitted.

"You haven't been yourself since Trouble and Jax ran away!" Mrs. Grimsby leaned toward her. "You haven't lost another cat, have you, dear?"

Miss Foyle's embarrassed silence was answer enough. Her neighbor looked out into the tall weeds of the backyard. "Cats are resilient. I'm sure they'll be fine." She patted Miss Foyle's knee again. "Still. Perhaps you should wait awhile before deciding about adopting another one, don't you think?"

Miss Foyle rose. "You are right about the bugs. Let's go inside and have that tea."

Mrs. Grimsby gave a sudden, nervous laugh. "Not in the parlor."

"Oh no," Miss Foyle said. "No indeed. Not in the parlor."

The grandmother clock downstairs chimed five times, echoing through the little house.

Miss Foyle awoke from her nap but kept her eyes closed, pretending she was still asleep. If she opened her eyes, it would know; she was sure; it would just know. Outside, a little boy ran down the sidewalk, calling for a friend to come out to play. The faint drone of an airplane rose and fell in a slow, gentle arc. Downstairs, dust motes drifted through the afternoon sunlight of the parlor. On the fireplace mantel, she knew, the blue cat glared in ruby-red fury.

Tink! Ting!

Her hands, folded across her stomach, clenched white. She couldn't help it. Stop, she thought desperately, uselessly. Please

God! Just …stop!

Tink! Ting!

She opened her eyes with a quiet sob, and sat up in her bed. Somehow, then, she gained the courage to stand. Somehow, she made her way into the upstairs hall, then down the stairs. Somehow—dear God! Dear God!—she entered the parlor, went around the settee, and approached the fireplace. Somehow, she raised a trembling hand toward the iron poker leaning by the ash shovel at the side of the hearth.

I will smash you! I will knock you to the hearthstone and break you into a thousand pieces! I will—

Miss Foyle cried out, jerking her hand back. Three of her fingers were cut and bleeding, each with four deep slices across the whorls of her fingertips. There was enough blood to run into her palm and drip in flat-sounding splats to the hearthstone at her feet.

"You are evil! Evil!" she screamed. "You are an EVIL THING!"

The figurine looked back at her with a sly grin.

Splat, another drop of blood fell. *Splat.*

"There aren't any more!" Miss Foyle sobbed, clutching at her hand, burying it in her chest. "I gave it back! You can't have it, you can't have any of them anymore, ever!" Her sobs ripped from her throat. "I'm done! I'm done feeding you!"

Tink! Ting!

She thrust her bloody hand forward once more, furious, beyond care, and again cried out at the new slashes of crystalline pain across her fingers. More blood, more droplets falling to the hearthstone. The eyes of the blue cat seemed to grow, to tilt, ever so slightly, laughing at her.

Tink! Ting!

Miss Foyle stood paralyzed, speechless, overcome with emotion and pain.

Tink! Ting!

She moaned.

Tink! Ting!

She swayed, but kept her balance. *Why can't I run! Why can't I run away?*

Tink! Ting!

Why can't I—

Tink! TING!

CRAACK!

Quite suddenly, the cat broke into several large pieces. They teetered on the mantel edge, then fell to the blood-splattered hearthstone below, shattering into a hundred, a thousand shards of glittering blue.

Miss Foyle, still rooted in place, stared open-mouthed. *What did I do? How did I…?* But she had done nothing, nothing at all. The cat, the insatiable, evil cat, had done it to itself. She moved, then, took a step back, then another, until she was out of the parlor. The remains of the blue cat lay scattered across the hearthstone like glittering diamonds. No, like…like simple, harmless shards of cheap blue glass.

The grandmother clock chimed ten times; time for bed. Miss Foyle went down the hallway to the stairs, passing the open doorway to the parlor. She felt a small blush of pride when she did not automatically look into the room.

She went slowly, steadily, up the stairs.

Her bedroom door was solid oak, thick and sturdy, and she locked it from the inside out of habit. She was safe. She knew that. Finally, safe. She cradled her bandaged hand, warm under the covers. This would be the first night, she realized, the first night in weeks where she could sleep without fear, without dread. She smiled in the darkness. Tomorrow she would clean the mess in the parlor. Tomorrow….

At some point in the night she dreamed: of darkness, tiny pinpricks of pain, a heavy pressure on her chest, and the stench of something rotted and foul, pressed to her face. *I am dreaming this,* she told herself. *I can dream away the weight, the pain, the smell; I can dream that I can breathe….*

She woke up, tried to draw a breath, but the weight, the

pinpricks, and the fetid smell were still there.

She opened her eyes.

To meet the ruby-red glare of the big blue cat sitting on her chest.

Turn of a Card

Earlier in the day, from his second-floor bedroom window, Mark's mother had pointed across the wide bowl-shaped valley of the town to the houses and trees on the far side and said, "There, can you see it? The grey roof...the one with the tower...that's the one we're going to see today." Like a toy, Mark had thought, squinting; a little place where ants lived.

Now, from the street, the house with the grey roof and the odd, cylindrical tower was...huge. It loomed, it soared, it rambled; it had more windows than Mark could count on both hands. He asked his parents, "What kind of a place is this, anyway?"

His mother squatted to his level and leaned back against the car door. "The style is called Queen Anne, hon."

"All those squiggly things on it makes it Queen Anne?"

She smiled. "All those squiggly things are called ginger-bread."

Mark's father cleared his throat. He said, "All those squiggly things are called a nightmare to whoever has climb a ladder to paint them."

"This house doesn't need much work at all," Mark's mother protested, rising. "You can see that even from here. It's beautiful, Dan."

"Now, maybe," Mark's father conceded. "But give it five

years, and you'll have me up there caulking and scraping and slapping on paint till the cows come home."

Mark unconsciously imitated his father's frown. "You don't want to move here, Dad?"

His father looked pointedly at his mother, then he smiled slightly. "We'll see," he said.

Coming down the sidewalk, a boy on a dayglo-green trail bike swerved to avoid them. "Hi," he said to Mark as he passed.

"Hi," Mark called after him.

The boy did a U-turn, and came back.

The two sized each other up, then the boy on the bike said, "You moving in here?"

"We're not sure." Mark glanced at his parents. "We're just looking."

The boy on the bike nodded to the house. "This is called the Briggs Place. The Briggs family lived here. For *years*."

"Must have been a lot of them," Mark's mother said.

"Nah. Only two, an old guy and his wife." The boy leaned close to Mark. "They died in there, you know. Died."

Mark's father chortled, but a quick look from Mark's mother silenced him, and he clapped his hand over his mouth.

Mark looked at the house again, his eyes wide with sudden apprehension. "Died? Inside the house?"

"In their beds," the boy on the bike said with finality. "There was an ambulance and police here and everything. First the wife, then the old guy a month later."

"Old people pass away in their sleep all the time, honey," his mother said. Then, to Mark's father, "Estate sale. We can knock ten thousand right off the top."

Mark looked at all the blank, shrouded windows; and the tower with its crazy conical roof; it was a creepy-looking house, after all. And now with two people actually dying inside it....

As though reading his mind, the boy on the bike said, "I'm pretty sure they haunt the place."

Mark's apprehension finally settled into his stomach as simple, cold fear...something about that house, something...

"Aw, you're just making that up," he said defensively.

The boy on the bike pointed. "Look at the place," he said. "What do you think?"

Mark's father cleared his throat as he stepped forward and gripped his son's shoulder. "There's no such thing as haunted houses, son."

"But Dad—"

"Listen, if this house is haunted, then I'm a…" He looked up. "What am I, Marion?"

"A monkey's uncle, among other things."

"Then I'm a monkey's uncle, okay?"

Mark looked at the house again—*haunted*—and swallowed. "Well…"

"Good afternoon!"

All four of them turned.

The real estate agent strode up the sidewalk, smiling broadly, her black plastic clipboard gripped firmly in hand.

"Hello, Joan," Mark's mother said, smiling back. "This is my husband Dan."

Mark's father nodded warily.

"Pleased to meet you at last!" Then the agent turned to the boy on the bike. "And hello to you too, Quentin Tolbert."

Quentin, saddled with his name at last, rolled his eyes.

The real estate agent lightly tapped his arm. "Are you selling another house for me?"

"I was just telling them it was haunted."

The real estate agent included Mark's parents in her quick laughter. "Kids," she said. She turned back to Quentin. "Now you scoot home and tell your mother I said hi." Then, extending the clipboard in the direction of the house to Mark and his parents, "Shall we?"

Mark trailed behind the grownups as they toured the house, but he never let himself be caught alone in any of the rooms. No use taking any chances, he decided, even though it was the middle of the day. A haunted house from the outside was bad enough, but when you were inside it…that was something else.

Something else entirely.

This particular haunted house was sneaky, though. There were no cobwebs, no old, ugly furniture with sheets draped over them; the wallpaper was smooth, the floors didn't creak, and the ceilings were only "fashionably cracked," as his mother put it, "And this woodwork, Dan! It's all original chestnut! We wouldn't have any stripping to do at all!"

This house was trying to hide its badness, Mark thought, but he wasn't fooled. With each room, with each passing moment, he couldn't shake the feeling of being inside a beast, a huge, evil, hungry beast, a beast just biding its time, waiting for the perfect opportunity—an opportunity on its own terms, not his—to swallow them up and never let them leave. Not alive, anyway.

Even on the second floor, where the large bedroom windows flooded the rooms with full, warm sunshine, the feeling persisted.

We have to get out of here, Mark decided, his uneasiness rising. We have to get out.

They finally ended up in a large bedroom with a curious circular room off one of its corners. Mark's mother gravitated to it immediately.

"That's part of the tower, of course," the agent said, beaming.

Mark's mother stood in the center of the little round room. There were windows three-quarters of the way around, looking out over the side lawn and the neighboring property. "This is exquisite," she said.

The agent followed her in. "If you think this is nice," she said, "then watch." She reached up, grabbed a metal ring on a chain hanging from the ceiling, and pulled. The ceiling blossomed, and a folding stair lowered itself gently to the floor at their feet. To Mark, it was as though The Beast had opened its mouth and extended its tongue.

She turned to Mark. "You want to go up first?"

He paled. "Uh…"

The agent held out a hand.

"Go on, Mark," his mother said, prodding him gently.

"Make the most of it."

Mark allowed her to pull him into the little room. He looked up the ladder stair and saw a flower-bud of beams in the ceiling of the room above, painted white. And sunlight. Tons of sunlight. It looked safe....

"Go for it, pal," his father said.

He glanced back to them, then put his hand on the smooth white rail and clambered up the steps.

At the top, he emerged into a room as small and as round as the one below, but here the windows went completely around, like a lighthouse. He could see the tops of the roofs of all of the surrounding houses, and into the tops of all of the trees.

"How is it, honey?" his mother called from below.

Momentary exhilaration surged: "It's...outrageous, Mom! You can see all over town!" He looked east, searching the far rooftops across town, and there, framed by the two sycamores in his backyard, he saw his own house. "Hey!" he yelled down excitedly, "I can even see our house!"

"All the way across town?" His father's voice was doubtful.

"Yeah! The two trees in the backyard and everything!"

"Well I'll be...darned," his father said, from below. Mark heard his mother chuckle quietly.

He lingered on his house roof for another moment, then jumped to others he recognized. The library, the drugstore with the apartments on top...even his school, with its big flag waving by the tall brick chimney ..

But then a stiff wind struck the tower, whistling under the window sashes, rattling the glass. He found himself looking down at the rooflines and gables of the house they were in, and a shiver of new fear suddenly coursed through him. He grabbed a window sash to steady himself, to stop it from rattling, and put his other hand to his mouth.

Up here. Whatever it was that haunted this house, it was right up here, with him.

I've got to do something! His head jerked about. I've got to do something!

He reached into his back jeans pocket and pulled out his pack of baseball cards. Unhesitatingly, he selected his only Chase Utley and put it quickly on one of the windowsills.

There.

There.

With that single, simple act, the house took a step back. He felt it. Like a vampire cowering before a crucifix, or a werewolf under a silver dagger, the house shrank away.

He stared at the card, amazed.

Then, from below, his mother said, "I think we should give this room to Mark."

Alone amidst the sky, the roofs, the trees, the magic, Mark held his breath, and thought, this is crazy....

The agent said, "Actually, this is considered the master bedroom."

But his mother interrupted, "I think a room with a tower just has to be a little boy's...don't you think so, Dan?"

Then, "Yeah," his father said. "Marko could have this room, no problem."

Marko. That meant his father was in a good mood. That meant....

Mark put his hand on his Chase Utley to draw from the power of its magic. Dad, he thought, you can't buy this house! You can't! The card got damp under his fingers, but he held on, and pressed...

"Come on down now, hon," his mother called up. Then, to the agent, "I think we're ready to talk. Dan?"

Mark held his breath again.

"Yeah," his father said. "I...guess it won't hurt to talk."

Mark opened his eyes, let his breath out, and lifted his hand away from the card. The magic was on its own, now. No matter what his parents said, or did, the magic would have to keep them from buying this house.

The magic would work.

It had to.

But when he reached the bottom of the ladder stair, he

found the real estate agent studiously examining the ceiling cornices with a quiet smile on her face....

While his mother kissed his father with abandon.

That night, an hour after Mark had gone to bed, his mother paused in the hallway outside his bedroom. "You still awake, honey?"

Mark shifted in the darkness. "I can't stop thinking about that house, Mom."

She came in and stood by his bed. "Well it's not our house yet. All we did was put a bid in. If they don't like our price...."

"You think they'll like the bid? You think we'll get it?"

She chuckled. "Honestly? I don't think so. I think it may be just a little beyond our means. Would it disappoint you if we didn't get it?"

"Nah," he said, as his heart skipped once, twice, "but I wouldn't want you to feel bad. I know you really like it."

She leaned over and kissed him lightly on the cheek, then went over to his window. "The air is a little cold tonight." She closed it.

Outside, through the trees, Mark could see the stars twinkling furiously in the wind, the same wind that had rattled the windows of the tower earlier in the day, the wind that had not stopped since.

At the door she paused again. "So you really like the house, Mark?"

"It's outrageous, Mom," he fibbed. "...Really."

She hesitated, perhaps sensing his lie, perhaps not. Then, "Want to go to IHOP tomorrow for pancakes?"

Mark grinned in the darkness. "Can I use all the syrups?"

"Sure you can."

He closed his eyes, "Sounds great, Mom." Then he yawned. "See you tomorrow."

"Sleep tight, honey." She closed his door softly, and the room filled up with night.

After a moment he got out of bed and padded silently over

to the window that his mother had closed.

He pressed his hands against the cool glass and looked out into the darkness. Somewhere, out there, was a house with a round tower, a tower full of windows, looking back. But it can't see me, he thought. There's no moon tonight, and I'm not going to open this window. I'm not.

The wind outside picked up, and the rushing sound of the leaves in the trees was like the roar of the crowd at a baseball stadium. Mark returned to bed, to the warmth that still lingered under his covers, thinking of the baseball card he had left on the windowsill in the tower, thinking of the magic....

C'mon, Chase, he prayed, do your thing, now....

The wind outside finally began to dwindle, and then to die. A bird in its nest awoke and cheeped sleepily, once, twice, then was quiet.

As he finally drifted off, Mark's breathing grew quiet as well, and soon his sleep was so deep he didn't make a sound.

The stars went slowly across the sky, the quietest of all.

Then a single gust of wind—abrupt, seemingly from out of nowhere—slapped the west side of the house. The trees in the yard roared once—

Mark's window opened.

The cold wind fluttered the pages of an open book on his desk.

Carried on the wind, borne by it: a flurry of tiny ripped pieces of cardboard, falling to the floor at the foot of Mark's bed. On one of the pieces: a portion of a dark red baseball cap, a piece of a forehead, and a single eye, staring out helplessly.

Slowly, slowly, the window closed.

Then, with a sound that only little boys could hear—little boys who *knew*, little boys who *believed*—something laughed.

The Wrinkle

"We need to send somebody who can shake the tree, some-one who'll take no prisoners." Ed Lewis's supervisor avoided eye contact. "Anyway, it'll only be for a few months. Six tops."

Ed looked at her like she had grown horns. "Six months in a hotel room?"

"Oh hell no. Employee Services is working with a local real estate office. We're getting you a short term rental, an apartment or a house, close enough to almost walk to the branch office. Or at least close to a bus route that'll take you there. City transit, easy peasy."

"What about Davenport? He can do it as well as me."

"Bill and Diane are expecting. Can't send him to a job half-way across the country with his wife having a baby, now, can I? You're single, no strings." She sat back. "Plus, between you and me, you're the best person for the job anyway, right?" She looked Ed right in the eye now, the lying bitch. The most expendable, she meant; the one we really don't need here at the home office. Six months doing a bullshit project in a bullshit field office. Six months, and then, for sure, a pink slip and a severance package to come home to.

"Right," he said. "Sure."

Sopwith Street was one-way, a solid block of rowhouses,

with parking only permitted on the south side of the street. Ed found a spot for his rental car only because it was mid-morning, and most people who lived there were probably at work. The address he had scribbled down during the realtor's last long-distance call was 1705. He cranked down the window and searched the porches and stoops for house numbers, finally finding a 1701 through the front door screen of one nearly across from him. He surveyed the house next to it and frowned, for there, on the riser of the top stoop step, he made out the nail holes and what looked to be the grimy ghost of 1705. 1701 to 1705? What happened to 1703?

"It'll need a little work, a little TLC," the realtor had said over the phone, "but we'll get the landlord to take care of everything, don't you worry, Mr. Lewis."

From what Ed could see, sitting in a hot car smelling vaguely of pine trees and piss, 1705 Sopwith Street hadn't even waved, let alone spoken, to Tender Loving Care in decades.

He got out, finally, and crossed the street. Standing in front of the sagging stoop steps, he glimpsed a boy, maybe five or six, looking at him between the porch spindles of 1701. Ed raised a hand, and after a moment the boy raised his, then climbed onto the railing and put his arm around the corner post.

"Hello," Ed said.

"Hi." The boy regarded him with serious, dark eyes. "You moving here?"

Ed almost nodded, but said instead, "Thinking about it."

"I wouldn't if I was you."

"Really? How come?"

"Cuz it's haunted."

"Really. This house? Ghosts?"

The boy nodded vigorously. "For real."

Ed put his hands on his hips and turned to take a serious look at this haunted house. Its porch was in the same sorry state as the stoop: the floorboards were warped and weather-stained, and everything needed repainting. The front window with its wavy glass looked original, and was probably drafty. The screen door screen was ripped in two places. The front door behind it had been painted a butter yellow at some point, but now its alligatored surface was almost grey. He turned back to the boy. "Really haunted, huh?"

"Yep."

"Ghosts?"

"For real!"

"But you live next door."

The boy gave Ed a look that said, "Don't you know anything?" "You have to go *inside* for the ghosts to get you. The ghosts are inside. They're not in *my* house; they're in *that* house."

"Ah," Ed nodded. "Of course." He put one foot up a step and leaned on his knee. "What's your name?"

"Bertie. Bertie Krukshank."

"Nice to meet you, Bertie Krukshank. My name is Ed."

A navy-blue Lincoln drove slowly past just then, and parked up by the corner. The woman who got out wore a smart pantsuit and carried a clipboard. The sun flashed off her sunglasses as she peered over them in Ed's direction. That would be Lacie, the real estate agent, who he had had a two-week-long telephone relationship with, arranging the move. She crossed the street, smiling, and extended her free hand when she reached the sidewalk. "Mr. Lewis! So nice to meet you at last."

"Call me Ed, please."

"I touched base with your employee services office before driving over. They said they would have the paperwork ready before the day is out." She gestured with her clipboard. "We just need to make sure this is the property for you, and then we just need to dot some 'i's and cross some 't's and get you moved in!"

This transfer to the field office is about to hit its first speed bump, Ed decided. "About that," he said.

"He doesn't want to move into a haunted house," Bertie said, still clinging to the porch post.

Lacie laughed. "What a sweet boy! I assure you, Mr. Lewis, there are no ghosts here."

Ed gestured to the house with outspread hands. "I'm a bit

more concerned with all this. I mean, if it's like this on the outside…"

"Our contractor is scheduled to have their crew here starting tomorrow. This will be all taken care of by the weekend. And the inside is already done. They did a wonderful job. Move-in ready. The furniture arrived just yesterday." She extended her clipboard. "Shall we take a tour?"

As she passed him, keys jangling, Ed said, "I almost approached the wrong house."

She turned on the middle step. "What do you mean?"

"The numbering. It skips 1703. It goes from 1701 to 1705."

"That's odd." Lacie consulted her clipboard. "This really is 1705."

"So there's no 1703?"

She looked at the house number through the screen next door. "Apparently not. They must have skipped it, for some reason, like you said."

Bertie nodded sagely. "Told you," he said.

Inside, upstairs, Lacie had just finished praising the afternoon sunlight in the front bedroom and the recently upgraded bathroom fixtures when Ed interrupted her. "What's the story with this?"

"This" was a doorway in the otherwise blank hallway wall, located halfway between the top of the stairs and the bathroom to the rear.

Lacie looked from the door to her clipboard, frowning. "Honestly? This is the first time I noticed that."

"There's a door between this house and the house next door?"

"Can't be. This is a firewall, like the one on the far side of the bedrooms. Solid brick." She frowned at her clipboard again. "How could I have missed that?"

He tried the knob. Locked. And residents, over the years, had painted over the door and surrounding trim so many times that the crack, the space between door and jamb, was solidly filled in with paint. "Maybe an old linen closet?"

"Can't be," Lacie said again. "Like I said: solid brick." She scribbled something on her clipboard.

He tried the knob one more time, then shrugged. "Did you say the shower head was a new one…?"

•

Back at the motel, Ed found the red light flashing on the bedside phone. He picked up the receiver as he sat, and pushed the button. "You had a call," the woman at the front desk said. "Someone named…" He heard rustling paper. "…Davenport? Said to call him back. Said you had the number." He did indeed. Ed dialed Bill Davenport's number, got his secretary Hazel, who said, "Let me transfer you," heard a beep, then another one, then *his* secretary Doris picked up. "Mr. Davenport's office," she said.

"Wow." Ed sat up. "That was quick. Bill's in my office now?"

"Mr. Lewis! Hello! Yes, well, they couldn't leave your position just open, could they? I mean–"

"Calm down, Doris, it's fine. You're there, I'm here; business goes on. Is Mr. Davenport available?"

"I'll put you right through. Enjoying your trip?"

Trip; that was funny. "It's fine. Missing you all, of course."

"That's sweet. Here's Mr. Davenport."

Click. Silence, then another click, and Ed was sure this time he had been disconnected, but then Bill's voice boomed, "Ed! Good to hear from you. What's up?"

"You called me."

"Oh. Right. Listen, do you know what happened to the Spillsbury file?"

"The Spillsbury file. Let's see. Last time I saw it, it was in the center basket, the one between the In basket and the Out basket, right there on my–on your desk."

"Well it's not there now."

"Maybe Angela in Fiscal borrowed it. She has her finger in that pie too."

"Angela. Huh. I'll check with her. Thanks. I bet you're

enjoying the trip."

Again with the trip. "Having a wonderful time. Wish you were here."

Davenport laughed. "Well, gotta go. You take care."

"You too." Ed hung up on a dial tone, smiling. He looked across to his briefcase on the dresser, next to the little black and white TV. He went over, opened it, and got out a seriously thick file. He hefted it, still smiling, then dumped it into the little trash bin beside the little room's little desk.

The neighbor next door, seated in a folding lawn chair on her porch, waved to him as he was fumbling with his keys while balancing a full grocery bag. "Hello there new neighbor! I'm Lori Krukshank. Can I help?"

"Hello. No, I'm fine. I'm Ed Lewis." The key finally slid home. "I met your son the other day. Bertie?"

"You must come back out and have some iced tea. It's such a hot day!"

Ed got the front door open. "Thank you. As soon as I put my groceries away?"

"Sounds wonderful! I'll bring it out. I have a pecan ring, fresh from Holtz's!"

Ten minutes later, seated on another lawn chair with an iced tea and a wedge of pastry, Ed said, "Your son Bertie is quite a boy."

"Oh dear! What has he done now?"

"Nothing. Nothing at all. He just told me he thinks my house is haunted, that's all."

Mrs. Krukshank rolled her eyes. "He likes to watch those old horror films when they come on The Million Dollar Movie, you know? Channel 9?"

"I don't have a TV, but I know what you're talking about."

"Bertie has quite the imagination. You wouldn't believe the things he comes up with."

A large, gunmetal grey Studebaker rumbled down the street, its driver searching for a possible parking spot.

"Do you have a car, Mr. Lewis? I only ask because street parking here on Sopwith is at a premium."

He shook his head. "I'm figuring out the bus schedules."

"The one on Frontier runs every twenty minutes. Takes you right downtown."

"I'll keep that in mind, thanks." He tried the pecan ring. "This is very good," he said, chewing.

"I'm so pleased. So how are you settling in?"

"It's fine. The house is fine. Everything is…fine."

"I only ask because we haven't had the best of luck with previous renters."

"How so?"

"They just seem to come and go. No one steady."

Ed swallowed another bite. "I guess you keep your side of the connecting door locked."

Mrs. Krukshank's forehead wrinkled. "Excuse me?"

"Upstairs, in the hall. The door."

"I'm sorry…" She shook her head slowly, still frowning.

He put his iced tea down. "The door through the common wall. The one between your house and mine."

"Through the firewall?"

"If that's what you call it."

"There aren't any doors through that wall, Mr. Lewis. No openings at all. It's solid brick behind the plaster."

"You're kidding."

She shook her head again. "So a fire in my house can't jump over you yours. It's like that in every rowhouse, I'm sure."

"Well, there is a door. On my side anyway. Really."

"How strange. Come!" She jumped up. "Let's investigate. You can show me where our door should be." She led him indoors and up to the second-floor hallway. She gestured to the featureless wall opposite the bedroom doors, a smooth expanse of geometric wallpaper. "See? No door."

"That's…weird." He went to the point nearly opposite the middle bedroom. "I mean, right here, on my side, there's a door."

"Well it can't lead anywhere, can it? It must be a false door, just for show. Have you tried to open it?"

"It's locked, and there's no key."

"Well there you go, then. A false door." She giggled. "*Faux*, as the French say."

Ed ran his hand over the wallpaper. There seemed to be nothing underneath, no outline of any kind. "Did you have this wallpaper put up?"

"No. It was here when we moved in, oh, ten years ago now." She felt the wallpaper herself. "I don't feel anything, do you?"

He knocked on the wall in several places; the sound was the same, solid plaster, solid brick. "No," he said.

•

Ed awoke in the night to a sound he thought he had dreamed, but as he lay blinking in the darkness, he realized he wasn't sure. After a moment, the sound came again, real, not in a dream at all: a door opening another creaking, squeaking inch. In the hallway.

Unlike in some B-movie plot, he didn't have a gun in the nightstand drawer, or under his pillow. He didn't even have a handy baseball bat. And the house's only phone was in the living room downstairs...

In the end he pushed the covers aside and, as quietly as possible, swung his feet to the floor and stood. He strained to listen, but now the house was silent. Only the outside sounds intruded: some neighbor's rattling window fan, the elevated all the way across the neighborhood, rumbling and squealing through a curve, all soft, all distant. The radium numbers and hands on the bedside clock radio glowed: 4:22.

He looked down the hallway from his bedroom door. His eyes were becoming accustomed to the dark enough to see that all three doors, the ones to the other bedrooms and the bathroom, were closed. The false door in the wall opposite was also closed, but it looked...odd.

He took a tentative step down the hallway, and then another, grasping the newel post at the end of the stairwell rail as he reached it. For a fleeting moment he considered just holding onto it, like clinging to a life preserver, something *real*, and not going farther.

But in the end he did: two more steps, to the door in the wall. Even in the darkness he could see that it looked...*new:* freshly painted, but with none in the cracks, and whatever light there was glittered off the new brass finish of the doorknob. How could that be? He had checked the door almost daily, in passing, running his finger along the paint-sealed cracks, grasping, if briefly, the worn pot metal of the knob. Always locked; always sealed; always *old*. How could it possibly be new, now? He touched the knob, grasped it, and then...turned it. As he slowly pulled the door open, it made the same creaking, squeaking noise that had awakened him.

He expected to see the solid brick of the firewall, but what he found instead was another upstairs hallway, a mirror-image of his own. It was illuminated by a soft, nearly indistinguishable light, as though a small lamp was on in one of the bedrooms. Was this the Krukshank's home? No; it couldn't be. Hadn't he run his hand over the wallpaper on their side? Hadn't he felt the solid, adjoining wall underneath? And hadn't their wallpaper been a regular pattern of lines and geometric shapes, not this riotous, old-fashioned floral pattern he saw now? No, this couldn't be his neighbors' house. However incredible it might seem, this had to be someplace else.

Turn around, he ordered himself. *Close the door. Don't, whatever you do, step across the threshold. Don't be crazy; don't be stupid.*

He looked into the other hallway, his eyes adjusting to the faint glow there.

A shiver of dizziness went through him, from head to toe.

"Eddie? Are you coming to bed?"

He startled, his mouth open. It had been a young woman's voice, coming from the front bedroom, the one at the end of this new, alien hallway.

"Eddie?"

He grabbed wildly for the door, slammed it shut, and ran

back to his bedroom. He slammed that door as well, and turned the lock.

My God, he thought, over and over, blinking in the darkness. *My God.*

He stared at the door from his bed, expecting to hear the door in the hallway open, and footsteps, and the voice of the young woman call out his name again as she knocked...

But nothing happened; no one came. The only sounds he heard were the ratcheting of the neighbor's window fan, the far-off wail of an ambulance, both set against the quiet murmur of a city still sleeping.

"The ghosts aren't on the outside," Bertie, the boy next door had said. *"They're on the inside."*

He finally got up, wiping sweat from his forehead, unlocked his bedroom door, and went into the hallway. The door in the wall looked a mile away. He went to it, stood before it, and reached out to run a finger down the paint-filled crack between door and jamb. Years of paint. Decades. He looked at the old, worn knob, but didn't dare touch it.

"Your house is haunted," Bertie said. *"For real."*

The clerk who delivered the requested files avoided eye contact. Ed wanted to stop her, to assure her that looking at him, even, God forbid, making simple conversation with him, would not cost her her job, but he watched her go, his smile wasted, without comment.

Later, when she returned with coffee, he wondered in passing if someone had spit in it.

Toward the end of the day, Mr. DeAngelo, the field office boss, knocked as he came in. He had a brave face on, a friendly grin. "How's it coming along? How's everyone treating you?" He took a seat opposite Ed, the grin remaining, like it had been screwed in place.

"I wish I could make this easier for you, Mr. DeAngelo," Ed said.

"You know what I wish?"

"What's that?"

"I wish I worked in a corner mom and pop grocery store."

Ed tried not to look surprised. "What makes you say that?"

"My greatgrandpop and my grandpop after him ran one, father to son, between the wars. On the corner, near where my dad grew up."

"Where was that?"

"A little neighborhood of rowhouses, just northeast of downtown, on the 906 bus line. Frontier."

"That might be near where I have my rental. I'm in a row house on Sopwith Street."

"Sopwith? Really? My grandpop's house was near there, on Magnolia. Now there's a coincidence!"

"Where was your grandfather's store?"

"On Sixth. Sixth and Magnolia. I think it's a bodega now." DeAngelo sighed. "Back then, every neighborhood had a mom and pop store, you know? I always remember him being a happy man, my grandpop. Just…happy."

"Those were simpler times," Ed said.

"That's what everybody says, but it's really just a catch-phrase. Life wasn't simpler, just…happier."

Ed nodded. "I wish I could make this simpler for you. Happy is out, of course." They shared a sympathetic smile. "I'll try to be quick, anyway. No need to drag it out."

"I appreciate that," DeAngelo said. "I really do."

Waiting with what had become the usual crowd at the bus stop, he felt himself wilting under the oppressive afternoon sun. Summers in Chicago were hotter, and more humid, but some days, he had found, this city gave Chi-town a run for its money. *I need to get a fan for the bedroom,* he thought, feeling a drop of sweat trickle slowly down his spine. *Just a cheap one, one I can leave behind.*

Sopwith Street had no trees, but his porch provided welcome shade, but inside, his house was a suffocating oven. "A change of clothes," he said aloud, as he trudged up the creaky stairs. "Out of this goddamn suit. And then a beer, in a frosty glass."

He stopped at the top of the stairs before turning to his bedroom. The door in the wall looked…different. He went to it, grasped the knob, and twisted. The doorknob turned.

The door was open again.

The sweat on his skin turned frigid, and he actually shivered.

"Eddie?"

He opened it.

"Eddie? Are you home already?"

He stepped through.

A young woman with soft, shoulder-length brunette curls framing a pretty face, and wearing a blouse, pleated skirt, and penny loafers, came up the stairs. Her laughter was like little silver bells, chiming. "Eddie! Why on earth are you wearing your best suit?"

He looked down at himself, then back up to her. She looked like she had stepped out of the 1940s. "I…I was at work."

"I know that! But in a suit?" She laughed again as she hugged him, and he smelled violets and talcum. She stepped back to inspect him. "I'm sure Mr. DeAngelo was impressed." She dusted something off his shoulder. "At least you wore your work apron, right? Tell me you wore your apron. Here." She helped him take off his suit coat. "Let me brush this and hang it up."

He watched her as she turned, her knee-length, pleated skirt flaring with the movement, and he saw seams running down the back of her exposed calves. Nylons? Who was this person? *When* was this person? She turned back with a coy grin. "Supper's almost on the table so you'd better wash up."

She walked by the open door without noticing it. He watched her enter the front bedroom. "The Clarkes are coming over later to play cards," she called back to him. "You have to promise not to cheat this time."

"I won't."

"Promise!"

"I promise. Cross my heart."

"I love you, honey."

"I...love you too." He hesitated. *I can stay,* he realized. *I can just go down that hallway, gather my young bride in my arms and kiss her. And stay.*

He stepped back through the doorway, into the dirty, sweltering shadows of his own hallway. "I promise," he whispered, and closed the door.

That night, well past midnight, he woke up needing to pee. His clothes lay in a rumpled pile on the floor. He felt a bit drunk, vaguely nauseous. What had he had for dinner? Nothing more than beer, and too much of it. *I need to eat better*, he thought, swinging his legs gingerly out of bed, pushing his discarded clothes aside. *I need to–*

Then he remembered. The young woman, her pleated skirt and nylons, the smell of her, all violets and talcum...a scarily vivid dream...

He reached down, grabbed up his shirt and smelled it. Talcum, violets...

He staggered upright, and ran into the hallway.

The door, that damned, crazy door, was closed, locked, and the cracks were filled with unbroken paint. Years of it. Decades.

What is going on? He turned about despairingly. *What in God's name is going on around here?*

Out of milk, and not wanting to deal with a bus ride to the nearest supermarket for just one thing, he decided to investigate the bodega on the corner. He stood on the cracked sidewalk, looking up past the plastered, haphazard printed signage and the neon "NEWS-CIGARETTES-BEER" sign, and could just make out another sign, a painted one, faded with time, and partially obscured on the bricks above, just a ghost, really: "DeANGELO's FRUIT & VEGETABLES," it read.

Paying for his carton of milk, he asked the middle-aged man behind the counter, "Do you remember when this place used to sell fresh fruit and vegetables?"

The man looked at him with a blank expression. "Qué?"

"Forget it," Ed said, and took his change.

The most difficult part of the job, the hard decisions, the winnowing, had begun at last. Ed reviewed eighteen personnel jackets in the morning, and by lunchtime he had separated out two of the jackets, and put them aside for further review. He locked the office door when he left.

Lunch, as had become custom, was a solitary sojourn across the busy avenue and down a side street to an old-fashioned aluminum-clad diner. Word had spread that he took his lunch there, so he was sure to be left alone. Ed Lewis the pariah. This day's special was Salisbury steak, mashed potatoes, and peas. He made sure to clean his plate, and he lingered over a second coffee.

Upon his return, passing a first-level supervisor's office on his way back to his own, Ed was called in with the busy wave of the supervisor's hand. They were on a first-name basis—keep your enemies closer, apparently—and this supervisor's name was Leonard. "Ed!" Leonard's smile looked nervous. "Close the door behind you and take a seat. How's it going?"

Ed hadn't reviewed Leonard's jacket yet, but he was on the list. Everyone was on the list, after all. "Only two so far today," Ed said, and to Leonard's next unasked question, "Bendix, and Shulman."

"Shulman!" Leonard's eyes went round. "Really?"

"Nothing's set in stone. It's my job, though."

Leonard nodded with a grim expression. "Better you…"

Returning, finally, to his office, opening the door, a piece of folded paper fluttered at his feet. Ed picked it up and read it.

YOU ARE A BLOOD-SUCKING BASTARD

He turned in the doorway. Across the hall, the racket of typewriters and adding machines continued unabated. Busy little beavers, showing him how well they worked, how important they were.

"You're right," he said, under his breath, crumpling the note. "I guess I am."

He stopped going to work. He called in sick once, then again, then stopped calling altogether. He also stopped answering the phone, and the doorbell. Whenever he found the upstairs hallway door open, he went through. Betty (that was her name, his young bride, Betty) was always there. His new life, on the other side of the door, was always waiting, like he somehow paused reality, between visits.

Finally, there came the day when he realized he was no longer visiting *here*, the world of Betty, of working in Mr. DeAngelo's store, but was instead visiting *there*, in a dirty rental house in a dirty little city, doing dirty work no one else wanted to do, a reality of disappointment, anger, and loneliness. *Here* was real; *there* was a slowly sinking, never-ending nightmare.

Betty made a joke about it, laughing, "You're always up here in the hallway! If there was room I'd put a chair so you could sit down." She hugged him, violets and talcum. "Come on now, or we'll be late for the Petersons' barbecue."

On his last day—he didn't know it was, but it was, nonetheless—Ed felt obligated to clean things up, just a little, just enough. He found he needed both hands to lug the trash can down the back steps. The screen door slapped loudly behind him. *I need to exercise more*, he told himself. He dragged the can across his postage-stamp backyard to the alley. When he turned, he saw the boy next door—Bertie—playing in his own little backyard, pushing toy cars and trucks through the dirt. "Well hello there," he said, coming to the fence.

Bertie looked up, squinting. "Oh. Hello. You're still here."

"I sure am." Ed gestured to the toy vehicles. "What's your favorite one?"

Bertie looked down at them, then back up. "Fire engine."

"I like that one too. Well, have fun." Ed started up his back steps.

"Did you see the ghosts yet?"

Ed turned and looked down to the boy, and shook his head. "Sorry to disappoint."

"They're probably in the wrinkle, then."

"In the what?"

"The wrinkle. The house in the middle. The *real* haunted house. You can't see it cuz it's in the wrinkle."

"But what's that?"

"What's what?"

"The wrinkle. What's the wrinkle?"

Bertie shrugged, "I don't know." His attention returned to the fire engine before him. "I just know it's there. I just know that's where the ghosts are "

Several days after hearing the last door knock, the last ring of the telephone ringing in the house beyond the door, the dirty house, the nightmare house, Ed paused in the upstairs hallway, hearing muted voices. They came not from downstairs, or from out the window, but through the wall before him. He heard stairs creaking as people ascended, and a voice he recognized, Lacie the real estate agent, saying, "...Three bedrooms up here, plus the full bath. The bath has a skylight, of course, like most rowhomes in this neighborhood."

Another voice intruded, "What about this door?"

They had stopped before the door in the hallway, directly opposite where Ed stood. He moved his hand across the expanse of wallpaper before him. Yet another voice asked, "What an odd thing. Where does it go?"

"Nowhere, really," Lacie said. "It's the firewall between the houses. Solid brick."

"How...weird." One of them tried the knob.

"Locked, of course," Lacie said. "It's even painted shut. See? Years of paint."

Downstairs, then, Betty called out, "Lunch is ready! Eddie?

Honey? Lunch!"

Had they heard that? He held his breath.

The voices continued down the hall. "As you can see, the toilet and sink have been recently replaced..."

Simpler. Happier.

He took one final look at the wall. The floral swirls of wallpaper was unbroken, seamless, flat. Just like it had always been. Just like it should be.

Downstairs, Betty smiled at him as he entered the kitchen. "Your soup is getting cold."

"I'm sure it's fine," he said, sitting down.

"What kept you?"

"I was listening to the ghosts."

"Oh Eddie!" She flapped her napkin open, and settled it on her lap. "It's probably just the new renters next door."

He surveyed the lunch his wife had laid out before him. It looked delicious. He began unfolding his own napkin. "You're probably right," he said.

Addenda

Journal Entries

4018 Ashburner Street
March 10, 1989
My three-year-old daughter and I were playing a game of
Candyland in the rear bedroom on the third floor of our house
on Ashburner Street. We were playing on the floor, next to the
bed. Behind me was the bedroom closet. I heard the latch of
the closet door snap open, and then heard the door swing out.
My daughter, who was facing the closet, looked past me with
widening eyes. Then the fuselage of a balsa free-flight model
airplane flew out out from its former location on the closet
shelf, sailed over both of our heads, and landed behind my
daughter by the door to the hallway. It made a perfect three
point landing. "Did you just see that?" I asked my daughter.
She didn't reply, except to nod slowly. Note: Today, she says she
doesn't remember the incident.

102 Norwood Road
January 21, 2015
Morning. I heard the sounds of two or more squirrels,
raccoons, whatever in the attic over the back bedroom I use as
an office. I checked the attic space—the attic only has the
trapdoor, no windows, no other way in or out—and saw no
evidence of rodents or animals of any kind. No holes, no
cracks, just the soffit vents for air circulation. I also did a visual
check outside, but the soffits all around were in place and
secure.

February 14, 2015
I was awakened at 4:10 am by the sound of something big and
heavy dropping to the ceiling joists in the attic, seemingly
directly overhead. A very loud thud. A check of the attic with a
flashlight found nothing. The blown-in insulation looked
undisturbed. There was about a six-inch layer of snow on the

roof, so when the sun came up I checked to see if any had slid and fallen off, or if some part of my roof had collapsed–it was that loud!–but the snow and the roof were undisturbed.

February 24, 2015
8:00 am. While working in my office room I heard another very loud thud from the attic, nearly as loud as the one I had heard a week and a half previously. A half-hour later came another loud thud from above. Out loud, I said, "Bring it down here."

My attic has two old, original interior doors that are positioned across the rafters for crawling on. The sound was very much like one of those doors being lifted, then dropped. The two original inhabitants of the house, from 1957 to the late 1990s, both died here. No one else has, to my knowledge.

June 25, 2015
4:55 am. I heard the distinct sound of a heavy step on the hardwood floor of my living room, causing the boards to creak a full three seconds. No other sound before or after. The HVAC was not on. This sound was so recognizable that I got out of bed and did a tour of the house, turning on all the lights and looking in all the closets, and checking the locks. Nothing.

October 14, 2016
Afternoon. From my living room I heard three knocks on the door in my kitchen that leads to the attached garage. One knock, then two more. The garage door was down, and couldn't be opened from the outside without the remote, and I hadn't heard the door opening anyway. I tried the door from the kitchen and found it was unlocked. This in itself was strange, because that door is always kept locked. I checked the garage, and found it empty except for my car.

I locked the door.

Credits

"300 Down," *The Porcupine Boy and Other Anthological Oddities*, Crossroad Press; 2019

"It's For You," *Cemetery Dance Magazine* #34; Spring 2001

"Killer," *Night Terrors* #1; June 1996

"La Hermanita," *Hog River Review*, Vol. 1; Spring 1973

"In The Stacks," *It's For You*, White Noise Press, 2011

"The Blue Cat," *SHIVERS VIII*, CD Publications; 2019

"Turn of a Card," *The Edge* #9; Spring 2001

The remaining stories and addenda are published here for the first time.

Bio

Keith Minnion sold his first short story to *Asimov's SF Adventure Magazine* in 1979. He has sold nearly three dozen stories, two novelettes, an art book of his best published illustrations, two story collections, and one novel since. Keith was a book designer and illustrator from the early 1990s to the 2010s, and also did extensive graphic design work for the Department of Defense. He is a former schoolteacher, DOD project manager, GPO Printing Contract Specialist, and officer in the U.S. Navy. He currently lives in the Shenandoah Valley of Virginia, pursuing oil and watercolor painting, joinery, and even some fiction writing.

Colophon

This book was composed and designed on an Apple iMac, using Apple Pages, and the Affinity software suite V. 1.7.3.

The text was set in Baskerville, Futura, and Marker Felt.

The interior artwork was created with watercolor and marker pen on bristol board, and soft pencil on coquille board.

The cover digital photograph was taken by the author.

Curious about other Crossroad Press books?
Stop by our site:
Http://store.crossroadpress.com
We offer quality writing
In digital, audio, and print formats.